BOOKS BY S. M. BOYCE

The Grimoire Saga

Lichgates

Treason

Heritage

Illusion

The Misanthrope

The First Vagabond: Rise of a Hero

The First Vagabond: Fall of a Legend

The Demon

The Fairhaven Chronicles

Glow

Shimmer

Ember

Nightfall

Standalone Novels

Ari

STAY CONNECTED

Boyce posts official artwork, updates, and random things that will make you laugh on Facebook, Instagram, and Twitter.

Boyce also created a special Facebook group specifically for readers like you to come together and share their lives and interests, especially regarding the Grimoire Saga novels. Please check it out and join in whenever you get the chance! Everyone in there is amazing, and you'll fit right in.

https://www.facebook.com/groups/Grimoire-Readers/

Sign up for email alerts of new releases AND exclusive access to the Grimoire Saga Fandom Encyclopedia: the official guide to Ourea exclusively for the Grimoire Saga's biggest fans. The encyclopedia is

ONLY available to Boyce's VIP email tribe, so sign up now to get access:

https://smboyce.com/email-signup-pages/gri-moire-saga/

Enjoying the series? Awesome! Help others discover the Grimoire Saga by leaving a review at Amazon: **http://mybook.to/misanthrope**

THE MISANTHROPE

BOOK FIVE OF THE GRIMOIRE SAGA

S. M. BOYCE

BOOK DESCRIPTION

Before Stone trained Kara Magari or taught the First Vagabond to master the Blood loyalty, he was nothing more than a slave boy named Terric.

Terric is a curious loner hellbent on reading his master's forbidden books. When one heist goes wrong, Terric abandons his old life and runs for freedom— only to fall prey to a ruthless man named Niccoli.

Niccoli is an isen—a creature of magic from the hidden world of Ourea—and he awakens within Terric an unimaginable gift. But this gift comes with a catch. Suddenly in control of newfound power he is forbidden to freely use, Terric realizes too late he simply traded one master for another.

In Ourea, a world dominated by the gifted, few isen dare defy their masters. Until now.

CONTENTS

For Geoff
I channel Stone through you. No wonder he's one of my favorites.

1

TERRIC

Terric's boots crunched through the snow. Frost bit at his nose, and white puffs of air left his mouth with each breath. Melted ice seeped through the tattered seams of his one good pair of shoes, soaking his feet. He shivered. He wore all four of his shirts for warmth in the late winter cold, but a blast of wind snaked through his collar. He rubbed his arms for warmth. Streaks of heat blipped in and out of existence under his hands, never lasting long enough to help.

He trudged toward his lord's manor to cook for the fat slob who had owned him since birth. His father had been caught stealing, and though the man and Terric's mother paid with their lives, Terric became a slave before he could walk. Seventeen years of cooking and hauling firewood were all he had ever known, and his only reprieve from the drudgery was stealing the lord's books one at a time.

A cook had taught him to read at a young age, and though she'd died years ago, she'd been the one person in this village he didn't despise. Though she had wistfully spoken of fanciful parties and a life of comfort, she had never told him where she had come from or how she had arrived at the lord's manor as a servant—though he had his suspicions it involved an affair and the vengeful wife of a powerful lord.

Pastures filled with cows and dung framed Terric's dirt path. Two young men his age laughed on the road ahead, shoving each other as they carried a bale of hay each to the fields. One caught Terric's eye, and the man's smile faded. He grimaced and tapped his friend's shoulder. Together, they broke into a jog as they headed out to the fields. The other boy never even looked over.

Idiots. They were slaves to the manor lord, same as Terric, even if they had the privilege of technically being serfs. He frowned. Still, most of the men could laugh—slaves and serfs alike. They slept with whatever women of their status would take them and seemed to enjoy at least some aspects of their lives. They had family, friends, lovers. Perhaps Terric was the strange one for hating everything he touched.

He almost laughed at himself. He didn't need friends. He had books.

And today, Terric would acquire a new book, the latest in the lord's collection—the *Anglo-Saxon Chronicles*. He smiled. Its newly minted leather had released an aroma as delicious as fresh bread when Terric filled the fireplace the other day, and he couldn't wait to crack open its secrets. For years, he'd daydreamed of worlds beyond what he knew—to think whole oceans of sand existed, or that somewhere, giant beasts with ivory tusks ruled the plains.

He smiled. He could escape from his shared, one-room hovel each time he slipped into the pages of his stolen books. Well, borrowed, really, as he only ever took one at a time and returned them as soon as he finished. To date, no one knew of his habit. The moronic manor lord never even read the things. They might as well serve a purpose for someone.

A hint of pine wafted past him, mixed with something floral he couldn't place. He paused, nose in the air, curious.

Something slammed against Terric's shoulder. He stumbled and spun around in time to find a man draped in a patchwork cloak made from brown squares. Its frayed ends dusted the frozen dirt, and its owner stared at him. Terric almost cursed at the stranger, but the intensity of the man's black eyes caught him off guard. He'd never seen this man before, and he seemed… off. With his broad shoulders and tall build, he appeared almost like the Vikings the cooks gossiped about during morning meals. His blond hair curled around a pointed face.

But the aroma. It sparked terror in Terric's gut, and it came from this man, radiating from him like heat. Terric savored the sweet scent even while it filled him with fear he didn't understand.

"Watch where you're going," Terric finally said.

"*Ya tebya nashol*," the man said, the words harsh.

Terric's eyebrows twisted with confusion at the unfamiliar words. He opened his mouth to speak, but the stranger turned and lumbered toward the one-room houses most of the manor slaves shared, his feet crunching in the snow. Terric frowned, curious about this new addition to the manor, but he resisted the impulse to follow. He was already late to the kitchens, and his book awaited him. He didn't need to chase a stranger around the lord's manor. He didn't care enough about anything the man might steal.

Terric resumed his march. The house's gray stones loomed closer with each step, but he ignored its thatched roof and glass windows. Its luxury bored him. He kept his eyes on the path until he shoved open the doors to the kitchens. A blast of air followed him in.

The cooks spun and raised their hands, speaking over each other at the intrusion.

"Close the door—"

"Idiot boy—"

"—you're late!"

Terric waved them away without reply and let the doors inch shut on their own behind him. A cook whose name he'd never bothered to learn brushed off her hands on her apron and slammed her palms against the wooden planks of the door, shoving them closed. A final puff of air slipped through, raising the hairs on Terric's neck.

"Late again," she said, clicking her tongue.

Terric shrugged and headed for the firewood pile. He knelt and picked up four logs, balancing them in one arm as he pushed open another door to enter the manor.

Time to get his book before the lord awoke.

A hallway stretched before him, lined with doors and portraits of the manor lord's ancestors. Men and women in frills and gowns stared down from the walls, watching him as he passed. Hardly useful sentries. His shoes tapped against the stone floor, echoing in the empty hall. He skipped the first three doors he was supposed to service and instead went straight for the library. With his free hand, he twisted the handle and slipped inside.

He scanned the room. Filled shelves ran along the

far wall. A fireplace between them. A wooden desk with spirals carved into its legs. An open journal on the table. An empty chair. He grinned, grateful the manor lord slept late.

Only two shelves flanked the fireplace, some of the books leaning against each other as they collected dust. But there, on the middle shelf to the right, sat the *Anglo-Saxon Chronicles.* Its brown leather cover leaned against a metal stand reserved for the latest arrival, and Terric sucked in a breath to savor the musk of its new hide binding. It tickled his nose and warmed his chest, lifting his soul for the few seconds it lingered.

He set his logs in the fireplace, careful as always to not spread the ash from previous fires onto the floor. He wiped his hands on the black streaks already staining his pants and lifted the book into his hands, savoring the caress of the leather against his fingertips.

A flicker of joy lit in his chest—his only dose, especially in winter. He slid the book into his pants and retied the drawstring to keep the tome in place. Once he went out to gather more wood, he would sneak back to his blankets and hide the book there so as not to ruin it with his chores.

He skimmed the spines in the shelves, searching for one of a similar color. He found a candidate—one he'd read twice already—and though its hue was slightly darker and the edges a little worn, he placed it on the display.

With his prize stowed away, Terric knelt at the fireplace and arranged the logs. He only needed to take one back with him, so he lifted the wood and placed it in his arm, same as he had when he entered.

Now, the hard part: leaving. A jolt of nerves shot through him, but he itched with excitement. His fingers shook. He reached for the knob and let himself back into the hall, barely allowing himself to breathe.

He had to make it to the kitchens, out into the snow, and back to his room without anyone seeing the outline of a brand-new book in his clothes. He'd done it countless times before because no one seemed to care about the worthless slave boy running errands. Each time, the nerves made his knees shake. And each time, he got away with it.

He straightened his shoulders and opened the door. In the hall, he shut the door behind him and began toward the kitchens.

One step at a time. Don't rush.

The book weighed on his pants tie, thicker than the others he'd stolen. It slipped a little more with each step. He gulped but leaned back a bit to compensate. A corner slipped past the waistband and poked at the fabric, as if trying to escape.

Terric lifted the book with his free hand and readjusted it, trying to move it back into his waistband. He eyed the door, ready to bolt back inside.

"You there! Boy!" a man yelled from behind him.

Panic rooted Terric's feet to the ground. He tilted his head enough to see behind him. Sure enough, a guard glowered at him from the far end of the hall, eyes on the book-sized bulge in Terric's clothes.

Sweat licked his palms despite the winter chill clinging to the walls. The book must have been too big for his usual ruse. He cursed himself. He'd been careless, too used to success to see the possibility of failure. His pulse raced as he sought an escape, but he had very few options.

The guard stomped along the hall, boots trailing clumps of mud every few feet.

"Careful not to get mud on the lord's hall," Terric said, hoping he sounded like the maids who cared about that sort of thing.

"It's worth a mess to catch a thief," the guard said.

He grabbed Terric's shoulder with one hand and lifted his shirt with the other to reveal the corner of a book peeking over his waistband.

The guard sneered, face creasing with what could only be wicked glee. "You know the penalty for theft, boy."

Terric swallowed. Dread shot clear to his toes, and a wave of fear crashed over him. He'd never been caught, but he'd seen others fail. Each earned ten lashings, or fifteen if the lord seemed angry. But in winter, with food scarce and little to keep him clean, the open wounds from the lashings wouldn't heal. They would grow green and black. He would fall asleep, moaning with fever like so many had before in this season, and he would never wake up.

Even if he did survive, he would never have access to the house again. He would never see the library or touch his precious books.

That wasn't a life worth living, and he refused to let the guard take him.

Terric lifted the log in his arm and swung it across the guard's head. The man cursed, and Terric slammed his heel into the guard's groin. The man fell to his knees, whimpering. The book clattered to the floor. Panicked, Terric grabbed it and ran for the nearest door outside.

He charged into the cold, shoes crunching once more in the snow. Fear propelled him forward. With every step, his eyes widened. His pulse echoed in his ear. Breath stung his chest. Panic drove him forward, and he obeyed its wild order to run.

No, think. Think!

The only trails he'd ever taken ran through the manor lord's forests. He'd never even seen the end of the man's property, much less crossed it. No other towns or manors existed near enough for him to have traveled there. A river ran along the outskirts of the manor property, but he'd never ventured beyond it. He'd never been allowed.

He needed to escape to the forests, and to survive

that, he needed food. He had a small stash of provisions stored in his bedroom, along with a second pair of shoes he'd acquired a year earlier when gambling with a farmhand who didn't know how to count. It had been too easy, and even though the shoes had rips in their soles, he kept his winnings.

Terric shifted course, aiming now for his shared room. He kept to quieter areas, avoiding the main paths and occupied pastures. He couldn't be seen. Too many of the fellow slave boys would jump at an opportunity to tackle him to the ground for nothing more than the recognition of their lord.

He reached the hovel and shoved the door open with all his might. It smacked against the wall, but he didn't bother closing it. He slammed the book on his blanket with a hollow thunk. A loose stone the size of his head sat in the corner, and he rolled it aside to reveal a hollowed cave hiding a worn pair of shoes, a handful of dried beef, and a frozen loaf of bread. He picked them up and threw them on the blanket, tied its edges together, and lifted it onto his shoulder. In barely twenty seconds, he'd cleared his meager possessions from the building and once more ran through the snow.

He cursed his timing. He couldn't have been caught in summer, no. He'd been caught after a fresh snowfall, where his prints would be easy to follow. He marveled that he'd been swift enough to escape the guards thus far. They had to know his path.

The wheels in his mind churned, desperate for an idea.

Avoid snow. Perhaps he could find a log and float the river. If the current moved quickly enough, he could—

"In here!" a man said.

Terric paused, heels skidding through the snow. He heaved, breath unable to keep up with his pace. The blond man in the patchwork cloak stood in the open doorway to the blacksmith's den, where the weapons were stored. No smoke churned from the chimney, so the blacksmiths must have not arrived yet for their day's work.

Eyes widening, the stranger gestured for Terric to come closer. A man shouted somewhere nearby. More shouts followed.

Terric's heart hammered against his chest. The stranger had no reason to hide him. He might even turn him in. He knew nothing about this person, but he also knew nothing about surviving on a floating log in icy waters during the late winter.

With a grunt, he obeyed. The man backed away enough to let him inside and lifted a hand, as if hailing someone. Terric turned, expecting a guard, but no one stood nearby. Instead, a gale blew past as he entered the hut, churning the snow. It teased his arms, lifting his hair on end, but trails of the white powder blew over his tracks as the door shut behind him. Though the gust seemed to have covered his tracks, he wasn't safe yet.

He spun to face his rescuer—or captor—and waited for an attack. He'd never seen kindness without gain, and it was only a matter of time before his new acquaintance revealed his intentions. Since the stranger had yet to yell for the guards, it was more likely he would hit Terric with one of the maces on the wall to knock him unconscious.

Terric prepared to duck and run yet again, but his rescuer stepped between him and the door. Instinct propelled him toward the exit, but a bulge the size of a beetle appeared in the stranger's temple. Terric backed away, eyes wide with horror. Skin dripped away like wax from the blond man's face as if an unseen knife were flaying him alive, but he didn't flinch or scream with pain.

"We lost the trail!" a muffled voice said through the door.

A gust of wind from some unseen crack in the blacksmith's hut chilled Terric clear to his toes, but his feet wouldn't listen to his terrified desire to run from the peeling skin before him. He didn't understand this man's changing face. He gagged as more flesh peeled away, falling faster with each second, his knees shaking even as a flicker of desire to study the change burned beneath the fear.

Within seconds, the stranger became someone else entirely. His face stretched into an oval. Black hair sprouted from the blond curls. His skin paled. A thin line of hair traced the jaw line and touched the man's lower lip.

An entirely new man wearing the stranger's cloak now stood at the door—the only way out.

Terric held his breath. Sorcery.

Even with all his books, he'd never read of a shapeshifter. These things didn't exist, and yet, one stood before him. Tricked him, even.

The stranger lifted his hand, palm up, and a gust of wind, much like the one that covered those tracks, hit Terric in the chest. He flew backward, head smacking against the stone. Something cracked. His vision dotted with spots. He slumped to the floor, and his chin fell against his chest as his world went dark.

2
SECOND CHANCES

February, 899 A.D.
Wessex, England

Terric woke to a sharp pain in his temple. He groaned. His head throbbed, pulsing as he fought to open his eyes. A drop of liquid tickled the crown of his head, its touch like frost on his skin. A shiver raced along his body, but his arms remained at his sides, bound by something wrapped around his torso. A gag covered his mouth.

He blinked and waited for his vision to clear. Brown and blue blurs seeped into focus. Rock walls composed a small cave. A lantern hung on a nail in the wall, casting its yellow light on the small room. Stalactites hung from the ceiling, and a few stalagmites littered the floor on either side of a tunnel at his feet.

Muscles tensed, he wriggled against the restraints. They didn't budge.

He leaned back to find the source of the liquid on his head, and a small pool of water met him. Its black depths teased the firelight, but the light danced along the surface ripples. He was dry, so he must have been dragged in through the tunnel—and therefore, it likely still housed his captor.

Terric took a deep breath, but he couldn't figure out how the hell he'd wound up in a cave.

With a pang, he remembered the blond man who shifted forms. The sorcery. He'd become a different person. Black hair. Oval face. Thin beard. Whoever that was, he must have dragged Terric to the cave and bound him. If he'd been handed over to the guards, Terric would be bound on the snow without a shirt, suffering his punishment for stealing from the manor lord. The mystery visitor had both saved him and restrained him.

But... why?

Terric grimaced. A gag and bindings meant trouble. Whatever this man had in mind for him, it likely wouldn't be pleasant. He didn't intend to stay long enough to find out.

He peered back over his head. To have water in the cave, he assumed a hole hid somewhere in its depths. His only questions, therefore, were where did it lead, would there be air, and could he escape?

With a few twists, he again fought with the binding around his body. It stretched, the knots loosening, and excitement shot through him. He twisted harder, legs lifting as he fought to free himself. But his body slid, and he sank an inch into the water. It now lapped at his hair, soaking him.

For fear of drowning, Terric relaxed into the bindings and frowned, trying to come up with a new plan. He could find a sharp rock to cut the ropes, perhaps, or—

Footsteps echoed down the tunnel, slow and steady. *Thump. Thump. Thump.*

Terric frowned and kept his eyes trained on the entrance, ready for whomever came for him.

Sure enough, the dark-haired version of the stranger walked through the tunnel entrance moments later. The man smiled, though his eyes narrowed, and a wave of nausea bubbled up Terric's throat. He suppressed the impulse to vomit and instead told himself to be calm and rational. A man like this probably didn't want to hear begging or pleading. He could shapeshift and control the wind. Unless those had been tricks, Terric would never be able to overpower his captor. Instead, he needed logic. He needed to finally apply his years of reading and isolation to something useful.

He scanned the man for clues. He wore a black shirt and jacket, clean and without a single patch on them.

No dirt under his nails. Smooth skin and trimmed hair. So, he was wealthy.

Terric frowned. That only raised further questions. What could a rich man want with a slave boy like him?

The man knelt at Terric's side, hiding any further clues, and removed the gag from around Terric's mouth.

The moment the cloth slid away, Terric asked the only logical question he could think of. "What do you want?"

In answer, the man looked at his right palm. Something appeared on his wrist and inched out like a dagger being pulled from a sheath. A thin, purple thorn slid from his skin and curved past his fingertips.

Terric's mouth fell open. More magic. His body shied away from the purple thorn in instinct, yet he stared with wonder. He'd never seen anything like this. It shimmered in the lantern light, almost as if it were wet. It fascinated him.

But the man didn't let him gape for long. He pushed Terric onto his side. Terric fought, wriggling in the man's grip, but a strong arm pressed into his shoulder and grabbed his shirt collar, rooting him in place.

Panic bubbled in his gut. This would not end well.

"Stop! For the love of—don't!" He couldn't keep himself from begging. He fought, surrendering his logic as instinct overtook him. He twisted his neck to see what would happen and pulled at the ropes, desperate to slide one of his arms from the bindings.

Something pricked the base of his neck, and his body stilled. A sharp pain shot from the wound, down his back, and clear to his toes. His arms no longer obeyed. His head slumped onto the wet bank. And though his eyes focused on the rock wall before him, they would no longer shift. He could smell the musk of moldy rocks, hear the lap of the water over his ear, but he could no longer control his body.

A hand pulled him roughly onto his back, and he once more stared at the ceiling. The man knelt nearby, only visible from Terric's periphery as a black blur with a pale face.

"Enjoy your trip," the man said, but with an accent Terric couldn't place. *Ehn-djoy yohr treep.*

The man dug his fingers into Terric's shirt and tugged, dragging him headfirst into the water. The liquid lapped at his skin, swallowing him with an icy slap. First, it covered his eyes. He stared through the surface, eyes squinting on impulse as the mineral water stung him. But then, with a final push from his captor, his nose and mouth slid under.

With no control over his body, Terric simply lay beneath the water. He couldn't move. He couldn't hold his breath. He couldn't scream.

Murder. The mystery man wanted to murder him.

Water rushed into his nose as his body continued to

breathe. He coughed on instinct, which only sucked in more. Pain exploded in his chest. It overwhelmed him, stealing away all other thought but the agony. His nose and mouth sucked in water like air, and his body shook as it gulped for more of what it would never have. He could only stare ahead and wait for death, aware of the danger but with no control to escape it.

Death, please. Death would be sweet compared to this. He wished he could even close his eyes, press them tightly together in his final moments so that he could have some control. But he didn't. His vision blurred. He stared ahead at the rippling surface, unable to see the rock ceiling anymore.

He thought back to his horrible and empty life. He'd done nothing. Achieved nothing. Was nothing. There was so much more to learn and explore and experience, and he would never know what the world held beyond the lord's manor.

Something popped in his chest. The agony receded. His vision faded, and all became black. A wave of relief washed through him as the pain lessened.

He floated in the darkness—no pain, no light, nothing. And in his final moments before even that disappeared, he managed one last thought.

This can't be all there is.

3

DEATH

Terric bolted upright. His head swam. He coughed and sputtered—anything to get the muddy bite of sand out of his mouth.

A pounding headache shattered his thoughts. He rubbed his temples, fighting to process what had happened. Thoughts swirled in his head, thoughts like *who am I* and *where am I* and *didn't I die?*

He opened his eyes, one hand on his head. A black stone floor stretched beneath him. Stalagmites protruded from it, pointing toward a dark ceiling littered with glowing blue dots. Stalactites hung from overhead, each a dagger threatening to fall at a moment's notice.

Terric set his hand behind him, and it slipped into water.

He flinched as the memory of his drowning came back in full force. He shot to his feet and stumbled into the wall, its rocky edges scratching him as he tried to get his bearings. A ripple spread out from where he'd sat moments before, but the otherwise still water reflected the glow of a thousand blue lights overhead.

The blue dots in the ceiling covered the walls as well, nothing but little crystals glowing from pores in the rock. Their blue haze lit the small cave. No doorway appeared between them, which meant he had no way out.

He ran a hand through his hair, struggling to understand. This cave had no exits, yet his tattered clothes were completely dry. He couldn't comprehend how he'd managed to even get here.

As he scanned his new prison, he noticed a figure standing in the corner. Terric jumped and pressed himself against the wall. Though shrouded in the shadows of the dark cave, the figure had skin as red as blood and wore only black pants. Layers of muscle pushed against the skin on his shoulders and back in an attempt to find space on his body. His eyes were all white, with no irises to them. This certainly wasn't the man who killed him, and Terric couldn't decide if it was human, either.

"Welcome," the creature said.

Terric glanced around the cave, and a sliver of realization snaked through him. "I'm dead, aren't I?"

"That is your choice."

Terric frowned. "That's not something I can choose if someone already killed me."

"On the contrary. You alone can decide whether you live or die in this moment."

"I don't see how that's possible. I'm fairly certain I drowned."

"You did, but you have a chance few others receive in life. You aren't human, Terric."

Terric squinted, brow furrowing as he fought to process the words. Of course, he was human. There was only the one option—human. What else could he be?

"You know my name?" he asked instead.

"You woke up in a room with no entry. Is my knowing your name so hard to believe?"

"I suppose not." Terric studied the white-eyed creature before him, but his gaze caught on the being's red skin. It reminded him of the devil preached about in sermons, but he'd never believed any of it. Angels and God and the Devil—they were tools to control the masses. They didn't work on him. Yet here he was, speaking to something not of this world. And it knew him.

"What are you?" he asked.

"I am Death."

Terric let out a breath, savoring the word as understanding swirled out of reach. Death. "And where are we?"

"The in-between. Your body is still alive, though barely. You may pass on to the next life or return to your body, stronger than before and with more power than you can imagine."

Terric's eyes widened. Life. Power. Strength. He could live again, start over. He could do something worth remembering this time.

"How do you know all this?" he asked, his voice a whisper.

"I am Death. I know all."

"So, you know how I died? Who was that man?"

Death nodded. "You were drowned by a man named Niccoli. All isen visit me at their first death and have the chance to return if their bodies are intact."

Terric paused, too many questions racing through his brain to pick only one. He chose the easiest one to ask. "But this man... what did he do to my neck?"

"Before he pushed you into the water, he pricked you with his barb. If you take my offer of a second chance at life, you will go back to him."

Terric paused. "But how is this possible?"

"You're not human, Terric. You're what's known as an isen, and your kind come back from the dead once in their lives. This is your opportunity to live again."

Terric gritted his teeth at the prospect of returning

to his old life. "But why bother? What I had at the lord's manor was hardly a life. If there's another world beyond this one, I'd rather go there."

Death shrugged. "And you can, but it is only fair to tell you of what you would miss in your old world. There is so much more to Earth than a mere manor slave's experience. There are mountains, warlords, alchemists. There is exploration, adventure, and more books than you could ever read in your life. Whole languages you've never heard. Castles you've never seen. There is a life there, Terric, and you can have it. All I need to know is that you want it. If not, I will allow you to die."

"And what's waiting for me on the other side?"

"I cannot tell you. It must be seen."

Terric frowned at the half-hearted answer. "Explain to me what an isen is."

"They are creatures of magic and longevity, and they—"

"Don't be ridiculous," Terric interrupted.

Death bristled.

"Magic isn't real. Science—"

"How did Niccoli shift forms, then?" Death asked.

Terric clamped his mouth shut and paused. Granted, he didn't have an answer.

Death crossed his arms. "And how did he shove you against a wall with nothing but air?"

Terric frowned. Another unanswerable question. "Do you know how it's done?"

"Of course."

"How, then?"

Death grinned and shook his head. "I am not your tutor. I am Death. I am a gatekeeper. You may stay or leave, but you must make your choice."

"You said yourself I should be informed. Inform me."

"Watch your tone, mortal," Death snapped.

A shiver raced up Terric's spine, and he gulped.

Death continued. "If you go back, you will have access to magic. You will learn what Niccoli did to you, learn how to control the energy of the Earth and live for centuries. You will excel. You will have a second chance at life away from the manor lord."

Joy swam in Terric's chest. "I'll be... free?"

Death paused. "In a way."

Free. Terric leaned against the wall and smiled. No more firewood. And power—he could master this magical nonsense. Understand it. Dissect it.

"Free," he said again, under his breath.

"In a way," Death repeated.

Terric plowed ahead, too excited to acknowledge Death's comment. "But the purple thorn in Niccoli's hand... what is that? And my body, how did it survive the drowning? What does the purple thorn do? What—"

"Enough," Death said, cutting him off with a wave of his hand. The creature pressed his eyes together as if he fought a headache.

"But the thorn is fascinating, and—"

"Boy, focus!"

Terric stood taller, feet rooting in place at Death's tone.

"Choose—a second chance on Earth, or a fresh start in the unknown?"

Terric sucked in a breath, lungs filling with sweet air. Freedom. He would live again, powerful and free this time.

"Send me back," he commanded Death.

"Very well. I will see you again someday, but for now, enjoy this second life," the white-eyed creature said.

Death offered his hand, and Terric stared at it for a moment, unsure of what he was supposed to do. When Death didn't budge, Terric finally crossed the gap between him and the creature to strike the deal. He wrapped his fingers around Death's hand. The warm skin almost burned him.

Freedom. He might have made a deal with the Devil, but Terric would finally be free.

4

FIRST SOUL

February, 899 A.D.
Wessex, England

Terric blinked himself awake, grateful his consciousness came without a headache. He sucked in a breath laced with the muddy crunch of the cave's stale air, but he didn't care.

His vision, blurry at first, gradually adjusted to the low-lit cave he'd died in. The same lantern burned on a nail by the entry. Dried sludge coated his neck, likely silt from the water. He rubbed it off and tried to stand, but his knees buckled. He sat again and took a moment to center himself.

He gulped in a breath. Life. How lovely. He'd actually come back from the dead.

White teeth appeared in the shadows of the tunnel.

Someone smiled, the light glinting on their off-white molars. The stranger stood and walked into the light, hands in his pockets.

Niccoli.

That bastard.

Terric pushed himself to his feet but fell yet again, so he pointed instead. "You. Explain. Explain why you killed me. Explain what—"

"Silence," Niccoli interrupted, voice still thick with an accent Terric couldn't place. *Sai-lehnts.*

Questions burned in the back of Terric's throat, but his mouth would no longer obey. His body relaxed, shoulders easing as he hunched in place. His limbs shut down, as if his body had obeyed Niccoli when all Terric wanted to do was badger him with questions—and perhaps a few rocks—until he finally had some solid answers.

"I am Niccoli." *I ehm Nikkolaih.*

Terric nodded.

"We are isen."

Terric nodded again.

Niccoli lifted his right hand, and the purple thorn extended from his wrist yet again. Terric sat up straighter, the hairs on his neck standing on end. He tensed, preparing to bolt if Niccoli tried to stick him again.

"This is the isen barb. It affords you immortality. With it, you steal souls, and they bring you eternal youth and life."

Terric's eyes popped. Death had called him a mortal, but Niccoli had promised him eternity. Perhaps, Death didn't have all the answers. Perhaps, Terric could live in this world forever, stealing whatever knowledge he could from Niccoli before he escaped and finally struck out on his own.

Freedom. It was so close.

"I am your master now," Niccoli said. *Ay ehm yohr mehstur nao.*

Terric frowned as deeply as he could. He was done with masters. But he thought back to how his body had obeyed Niccoli's silent command, and dread sank into his toes. Perhaps—no, it couldn't be. No one could control another's body. Not even magic could do that.

Could it?

"Are you good at anything?" Niccoli asked.

Terric cleared his throat. "I can read."

"Good, good. What else?"

"I enjoy learning. War theory. Science."

Niccoli grinned, though his eyes narrowed once again. He studied Terric, and each smile seemed nothing more than a silent victory. As if Terric had shown his cards without realizing it. As if Niccoli had the upper hand yet again.

"You are a studious man, would you say?" he asked.

Terric flicked a pebble into the water. "As far as a slave can be."

"Explain this."

Niccoli extended his palm, and a fire roared to life above his fingers. It flickered, orange and brilliant enough to cast his shadow along the floor.

Terric's mouth fell open, and he leaned in. Heat radiated from the flame. It cast an orange glow, same as every other fire he'd seen in life. Yet it floated in the man's hands, suspended as it consumed nothing but the air. He reached for it, looking for the trick, but the fire singed his fingertip. Agony rippled through his body. He yelped and shook his hand to dull the pain. Rivets of pain raced down his fingers, aching with each beat of his heart.

Niccoli laughed, and the fire sputtered out. Only his unscathed hand remained. "Not everything is meant to be understood. Magic is one of those mysteries of life you will never dissect."

Terric huffed in annoyance. Although Niccoli's eyes narrowed in what could only be warning, Terric disagreed. If he was to live in this world with magic, he would understand it. He would master its secrets and determine how it worked.

Terric nodded to the man's empty palm. "Will you teach me?"

Niccoli stood. "In good time. For now, there are more pressing things to learn. First, do you have any problem with stealing a soul?"

"What does that mean?"

"You acquire the soul, and with it, its gifts, powers, and knowledge. You must steal a soul every ten years to maintain your youth and longevity. It will remain with you for your life."

Terric shrugged. "It depends on the soul, I suppose."

Niccoli clicked his tongue and shook his head. "I found a soul for you to start with."

Concern burned in Terric's gut. He didn't like the sound of that.

Niccoli walked through the tunnel entrance and disappeared with a gesture for Terric to follow. Terric remained in the cave, testing whether or not his feet would follow on their own. They didn't. He straightened his tunic, stood tall, and followed Niccoli into the shadows.

The tunnel curved for a few seconds before light bled into existence around a corner. Rays cut through the gloom, slicing shadows like a sword through a body. But as Terric rounded the bend into the light, it assaulted him. His world went white. He squinted and held an arm over his eyes as they adjusted.

Something pinched the tender skin underneath his right wrist. He flinched and touched the area with his free hand, searching for the culprit. A thorn protruded from him, its base slick with a thin coat of slime. He lowered his arm to examine it, eyeing the purple thorn as it curved to his fingers like a dagger he could stow within his body. He shuddered. Perhaps, this had always been a part of him, and he'd simply never known. He'd never felt it before, yet here it was.

He had to know if it had always been there. Perhaps he could experiment on other isen before their trip to Death, or—

"Terric," Niccoli snapped. *Terreek.*

Terric looked again at the exit, and the light stung his eyes once more. He blinked away the burn and waited for his vision to clear, studying the hall as it came into view. The tunnel ended about twenty steps away. Niccoli had already exited the cave and stood at a tree framed by the cave's entrance. A second man knelt at the trunk in the black tunics and pants of the manor lord's guards, his arms bound with ropes wrapped around the tree. A gag had been tied around his mouth, and the knot bobbed as he shook, head down.

Terric paused, not curious in the slightest. He didn't want a worthless guard's life. If he were to steal a soul, he wanted a scientist. A linguist. Someone useful.

The guard's head turned, and Terric recognized the man who caught him with the book in his pant's lining.

"I thought you would enjoy a bit of revenge," Niccoli said with a smirk.

"No, thank you," Terric replied.

Niccoli's smile fell, and he pointed at the guard. "You will steal his soul, you will do it now, and you will thank me."

Terric stood straighter. He should be a free man

now, not answering to a stranger's whim. He'd done that for seventeen years. He wouldn't do it again. "I would prefer to take a useful soul when I'm ready, not this garbage."

Niccoli's eyebrows dipped as he scowled. "Absorb his soul."

Terric's legs obeyed even as he fought the command. They trotted to the tree and knelt. His right hand, its purple barb still extended, hovered over the guard's neck as if Niccoli himself had placed it there. Terric didn't even know if the soul could be housed in the spine, or if that was merely a means of connecting two isen before one of them was sent to his first death. The guard whimpered and squeezed his eyes shut.

"I don't even know how to do this," Terric protested.

"Stab here," Niccoli said, tapping the man at the base of the neck. The guard flinched at his touch.

"But—"

"Now!" Niccoli commanded.

Terric's hand moved on its own, and the purple thorn slid into the man's skin. Terric shuddered, and a wave of displeasure rippled down his spine. It was as if his skin wanted to escape his body, to get away from the horrible thing he'd done and barely understood. The guard screamed, but it trailed off with a gurgle.

The world faded to black, and gray shadows twirled

through the darkness. The last thing Terric saw was the knot of the guard's gag bouncing as the man twitched.

In the swirling darkness of wherever he'd gone, the guard appeared again. Still bound, he faced Terric with bloodshot eyes. His skin began to gray, and flakes of it fell off here and there—rather like Niccoli's had when he transformed from the blond man to what Terric assumed was his natural, dark-haired form. But instead of changing his face, the guard turned to wax at Terric's feet.

A rush of knowledge flooded him—things he didn't care to know but was forced to digest regardless.

Chad. The guard's name was Chad.

Terric resisted the connection bridging between him and Chad. He didn't want this soul. He already knew it would be worthless. A waste. Perhaps he could release it somehow, or—

But Niccoli's command overrode his thoughts. *Steal this soul. Now!*

A shiver raced along Terric's skin, followed by a wave of disgust.

Flashes of Chad's life blurred across Terric's vision, blipping in and out of existence like a moving portrait over the black recesses of wherever they'd escaped to.

Chad is five. A man raises his hand to strike him—Father. Father is so tall, so big. This will hurt.

The palm comes down across Chad's face, and he falls to the floor, sobbing.

"Be a man," Father says. He walks outside, pushing past Mother. She stumbles into the wall, her pregnant belly smacking the doorway. She cries in pain, and Chad joins her, his sobs louder than hers.

Terric huffed. "Be a man," indeed.

Another moving portrait flashed in the darkness. He groaned. Not another one. He didn't care. He wanted this to be over.

Chad pushes a small boy into the mud. Chad is big for his age, and he can shove the other boys around with ease. They all shiver like little girls around him. Chad likes it.

"Be a man," Chad says, laughing. Two other boys laugh with him. They run to find another victim and another puddle of mud.

The portrait dissolved, and in the still-twirling blackness, Chad's adult form lay slumped over Terric's feet. His skin gray, Chad looked straight ahead. He no longer blinked or shivered in fear. He lay still as a stone.

Another moving image appeared, and Terric ran a hand through his hair in frustration.

Chad runs his hand up the thigh of a woman in a tavern. Her dark hair spills over her shoulders and touches the open collar of her dress. With a bust like that, she must have been begging for this.

She pushes against him. "Stop it!"

He shoves her against the wall. She presses her palms against his chest, twisting in her futile efforts to get away.

"Enough, enough," Terric said, waving his hand at the image. It dissolved.

Good. At least he had some say in the matter.

Another portrait popped up, and he almost waved it away as well—that was, until he saw himself from Chad's eyes.

The quiet slave boy stands at the library door, eyes darting around. Pitiful. The outline of a book pushes against the boy's pants, the clear square a dead giveaway for a thief. What an idiot.

Self-loathing and shame swelled in Terric's gut. The bulge of a book in his pants was painfully obvious from this perspective. He'd been easy to catch. Stupid. Foolhardy. What an idiot, indeed.

He waved away the image, and none flitted forward to replace it. Terric grimaced at the gray figure at his feet—a waste of life. Chad had savored the misery in others. It disgusted Terric to think he was stuck with this soul in his head for the rest of his own life. He would try to bury Chad deep in his mind or wherever souls were stored. He wished for this useless man to be hidden forever, a shame buried deep in the darkness. But given his lack of control in stealing the soul to begin with, Terric doubted he would succeed in suppressing it.

The shadows brightened. Chad's body faded until it disappeared in the growing light. Bits of color popped into view— brown branches, the gray-blue of a winter sky—until he stood once more at the base of the tree. Chad's body slumped against the trunk, still tied with Terric's purple thorn in the base of his neck.

Terric withdrew the barb. It slurped. A hole appeared where it had nestled into his prey, and blood spilled from the wound. It dribbled over the guard's skin and bled into his black tunic.

"Marvelous," Niccoli said, clapping from his seat on the grass nearby. *Marrveelos.*

Terric tried to shake his master's accent from his mind. And master he was; he'd forced Terric to consume a soul he didn't want. It was worse than being a slave to the manor lord. With the lord, at least he could defer tasks he didn't like to someone else. He could barter chores, and he negotiated well. He did the barest minimum to stay under the radar. But not with Niccoli. With the isen master, Terric was a true slave, one who could be forced to obey, whose will could apparently be manipulated.

In his second life, Terric had done nothing more than trade his original master for a worse one.

A memory of Death's voice rang in his head. "You will be free… in a way." That creature had all but lied. He wished he could throttle that red neck, watch those white eyes bulge. He gritted his teeth and clenched his fists, wishing for a way out.

His purple thorn wouldn't retract. He needed it gone. He didn't want to look at it or think of what he'd become. Once more, he disgusted himself. He should have gone to the next world. Started over.

"What did you learn?" Niccoli asked.

Terric stared at his master, probably glaring. He didn't care. The isen didn't flinch or frown. Terric didn't seem to faze him.

"Well?" Niccoli prodded.

"I have no control over myself. I'm your slave."

Niccoli clicked his tongue. "Harsh words. Do as I say, and you will have freedoms. Disobey, and I will make your life very," he grinned, eyes narrowing, "painful. But what did you learn from the soul?"

"Nothing. It's worthless."

"Ah, no soul is worthless. Even with slime like this man, there is something to take—be it wisdom, a lesson, a power, or a gift. At the very least, you can change into his form. You could infiltrate the manor again. There are options. You will discover his use over time."

Niccoli stood and walked into the woods with a gesture for Terric to once more follow. Terric grunted. Follow. Obey. Agree. He hadn't faced Death to become a slave a second time. Whatever the costs, he would shake Niccoli's grasp on him. He would escape. And someday, Terric would be free.

5

A NEW NAME

February, 899 A.D.
Wessex, England

Terric plodded along behind Niccoli, heels barely leaving the ground as they left the cave—and Niccoli's lantern—behind. He had to follow his master, but he didn't have to enjoy it. They crunched across the snow, marching through a forest Terric had never seen. Trees crowded together, most of them bare of their leaves. Naked twigs poked the sky above.

"Where are we going?" Terric finally asked.

"Back to camp." *Behk tu kehmp.*

Terric wished he could place his master's accent. Each word nestled in his ear like a bug, waiting for him to guess the right language of origin. But he'd only ever known English.

Footprints appeared ahead in the snow, trails made by other people weaving in and out of the trees.

"Are there others?" Terric asked.

"Yes."

He waited for more, but no explanation came. Evidently, he would have to find out when they arrived.

More footprints littered the snow. The trees thinned, and occasional conversations drifted through the woods. Sheets hung over branches and were tied to the ground with ropes, the fabric fluttering and shaking loose frost with each gust of winter wind. Smoke wafted upward from behind a clump of trees. Warmth. Terric rubbed his hands together, eager for a chance by the fire.

A woman walked past, a basket on one hip. She turned and nodded to Niccoli without a glance to Terric.

"Mirina," Niccoli said with a nod of his head.

Mirina continued toward the smoke. Nerves clawed at Terric's gut, but he pushed them away. He couldn't expect courtesy from isen, not if Niccoli had kidnapped and enslaved all of them as well. They wanted to be here as little as he did. They were prob-ably looking for a weakness, a chance to escape, same as him. He'd never needed friends before. He wouldn't start now.

He did, however, want some books.

"What did you do with the book in my blanket?" Terric asked.

Niccoli grinned, those off-white teeth flashing. "If you behave, I will let you read it."

Terric frowned. "It's my book."

"No, it is the manor lord's' book. You stole it." *Yu stohl eet.*

Terric rolled his eyes and studied the forest. "What do I have to do to get it back?"

"Obey."

His fists tightened. He opened his mouth to speak, to disagree, but a louder conversation interrupted Terric's thoughts. Chatter bubbled over the quiet forest, chasing away whatever wildlife still inhabited the woods. Another woman, this one with blond hair, walked across the field toward a tied sheet, her exposed hands pink with cold. A blond man as broad and tall as Niccoli had been before he'd shifted form ducked beneath another sheet and crouched on the ground, rubbing his hands.

The fire appeared as Terric passed yet another sheet. A dozen people crowded around it, talking or stirring pots over the flame. Terric straightened and quickened his pace, eager to reach the fire.

"Good afternoon," Niccoli said, voice clear as a bell

over the din.

Voices hushed, and all of the faces turned toward them. Many eyed Terric, their eyes passing over him with fleeting glances. He'd apparently earned nothing but mild interest in this group of supernatural beings.

That suited him fine. If all went well, he wouldn't be with them long.

A few of the folks by the fire nodded to Niccoli in welcome and greeted him with hushed voices. All but one. A tall man on the opposite side of the fire stood and towered over the rest. His dark hair framed a smiling face and curled around his head, loose and curvy like a Viking—at least according to the rumors Terric had heard.

"Niccoli, welcome back!" the man said, voice booming. Terric almost flinched, he was so loud.

Niccoli set his hand on Terric's shoulder. As much as he wanted to, Terric resisted the urge to shove it away. True, he hated the man and his touch, but he had to at least pretend to obey. He didn't know how to charm others, but he could lie and play along. That would suffice. Terric would get his book. He would learn what he could from Niccoli. And when he'd used up his master's knowledge, he would escape.

"Boy, these are my children." Niccoli gestured to the people by the fire.

Terric eyed the varying heights and facial features, convinced Niccoli hadn't fathered a single one of them.

The tall man with raven hair laughed, as if he'd read Terric's mind. "Not his *real* children, mind you. It's an isen term. He turned us, and we are, therefore, his children."

Terric pursed his lips. That was a stupid term to choose.

"He has the charm of a block of stone, Niccoli," the raven-haired man said with a grin.

Niccoli laughed. "This one is defective, yes, but far smarter than any of you."

Two women by the fire sniffed and turned up their noses, and another man sitting by the flame shook his head before dipping a ladle into a black caldron suspended on metal stakes over the flame. Several others turned away.

Terric suppressed the desire to roll his eyes. Excellent. Now they all despised him a little, rather than simply ignoring him. It didn't matter. He was, most likely, smarter than most of them.

Niccoli gestured to the tall man with black hair. "Andor, find the boy something to eat."

Andor sat down once more and gestured for Terric to join him. "We have bread and some venison. Maybe a carrot if you're lucky."

Terric sat beside the massive man and took the metal plate he was given. A hunk of brown meat sat on the dish with a piece of bread the same shade. No carrots, but Terric didn't care. He grabbed the meat with his fingers and tore into it, grateful for the first bite of sustenance since his ordeal with Death. The hearty warmth filled his mouth, and he closed his eyes with pleasure.

Andor chuckled. "Mirina will be pleased to know someone at last enjoys her cooking."

Terric grunted in reply and bit into the bread. It scratched his throat, but he swallowed it regardless.

"When did Niccoli awaken you?" Andor asked.

"This morning."

"And he brought you back already? He's been gone for four days, so... no, it doesn't matter. I guess we'll be leaving soon."

Terric shrugged and took another bite of meat.

"Look, Sir Stone, a conversation is meant to have two participants, not one."

He frowned but didn't look up from his meal. "My name is Terric, not Stone."

"I notice you don't have a weapon, Stone." Andor said with a grin, emphasizing the last word.

"It's Terric."

"You'll have to learn to fight, you know. Never fear, boy. I'll teach you."

Terric set his plate on his lap and faced Andor, only to see the man's head towering a good foot and a half above his even though they both sat on the same log. The man was huge. His shoulders were twice as wide as Terric's, and though he hated Andor's nickname for him, he realized with a sudden pang of dread that there was nothing he wanted to do about it. Not at the risk of getting Andor's giant fist to his face. At the manor, he'd lost too many fights he never started. He didn't dream of starting one with a creature that had faced Death and come back, even if he was one of them now.

"Thank you," Terric eventually said, not entirely remembering what had been offered.

Andor's smile widened. "Now, have you heard much of Ourea yet?"

"Of… what?"

"Nothing at all? I guess I can't be too surprised. There's too much to understand after you speak with Death and steal the first soul."

Terric pushed the last bite of meat around on his plate, appetite fading as he recalled Chad's sobbing form slumped at the base of the tree. "Who was your first soul?"

Andor grabbed a stick and poked the fire. "A fellow Viking."

"So, you're a Viking? I figured as much. You're massive."

The Viking laughed and poked the fire. "I like that you don't pry."

"What are you talking about?"

Andor laughed again. "See? Anyone else would ask what the Viking did, or why he was my first soul. They'd want a story. But you don't care, do you?"

"Not particularly," Terric admitted.

Andor burst into laughter, but Terric didn't understand why. "Funny, boy. You won't fit in at all in Ourea. Or here, for that matter. You're an oddity."

Terric already knew that, but he didn't know about this place Andor kept mentioning. "Tell me more about Ourea."

"I haven't been yet, but I hear it's full of magic and monsters. Creatures of your nightmares and that kind of thing. I've been shadowing an elder isen, one of Niccoli's first children, and he's told me stories. It's sorcery, all of it. Creatures with six legs and dagger-long fangs, taller than a horse. Eagles with the body of a cat and long tails. There are even races called yakona that look like us and have mastered magic. Steal one of their souls, and you'll have powerful gifts for life. I'm holding out for one of them for my next soul. I want to learn magic."

Terric's mind raced. He tried to picture these creatures, but nothing in his limited experience could inspire him. He'd read little about mystical creatures in his stolen books, and even less about magic. To experience them for himself—now that was worth facing Death itself.

He leaned toward Andor. "Have you learned any magic yet? Niccoli showed me a flame in his palm, but I couldn't figure out how he did it."

"Not even a little. All in good time, though. We have forever, after all."

A flicker of glee erupted in Terric's chest. Yes, he did have forever. "Are we going to Ourea?"

Andor nodded. "Niccoli has a mansion there. That's home. He's been growing his guild—that's what a family of us isen are called—and every now and again, he sends his new children back with an elder isen who knows the way. It's about time. We have a sizeable group already."

"But how do we get there? What is the manor like? Does it have a library? Does—"

Andor laughed. "Slow down, Sir Stone. All in good time. For now, eat up."

"It's Ter—"

A woman giggled from across the fire. "Yes, finish your food, Stone. Can't waste."

Terric grimaced at the nickname, but she smirked. She'd done that on purpose, the little idiot.

"I like that name for you," Niccoli said from behind him.

Terric twisted in his seat and tensed. His master stood a few feet off, arms crossed. Several of the men and women around the fire snickered.

Niccoli grinned. "It's a new life. You should have a new name. Stone it is."

Terric sucked in a breath and returned to his plate,

closing his eyes to keep himself from saying something stupid.

Play along.

"Are we leaving soon?" Andor asked.

Niccoli nodded. "Pack up. We're leaving now."

"To Ourea?" Terric asked.

In his periphery, he noticed several heads turn toward him. No one spoke, everyone apparently waiting for the answer.

"To Ourea," Niccoli confirmed.

A pang of joy leapt in Terric's chest. Ourea was a world of magic. He could finally study it, learn how it worked, and—

"You and I will continue to Paris," Niccoli finished.

Terric spun around to find his master staring at him, and dread replaced his joy. He didn't want to wander around Earth as Niccoli's slave.

"Why?" he asked.

Several women gasped. All eyes flitted to Niccoli, and the camp seemed to hold its breath while it awaited his answer.

"Because you do as you're told."

A tug on Terric's gut brought him to his feet, and his plate spilled onto the ground. Behave. Obey. Niccoli must have overpowered his will once again, only without speaking this time, and commanded him to do what he didn't want to do.

Niccoli wanted to watch him. To make sure he

obeyed. Terric had stolen from the manor lord, so what was to stop him from stealing from Niccoli, or escaping? He understood now. Terric was a risk, one Niccoli would keep close. Until Terric could smile and obey like Andor, he would be at Niccoli's side.

He all but groaned. If that were the case, he would be at Niccoli's side forever.

"Pack!" Niccoli ordered, eyes scanning the stunned crowd. Many flinched, and several hurried away. Others collected the pots, while Andor kicked snow over the fire.

Terric reached for his plate and caught Andor's eye. The Viking paused, but eventually turned and walked toward one of the sheet tents not far off.

Rescue came for princesses, not slave boys. Terric clenched his fist, not quite sure what he'd hoped Andor would do. If he wanted to escape Niccoli, he would have to do it himself.

Someone whispered in his ear. He spun around, but the nearest man stood ten feet off. The voice sounded again, quiet and familiar. He hesitated, trying to place the voice, and the realization hit him like a ball of snow to the face—the guard. Chad's voice echoed in his ear, distant and desperate.

He swallowed hard and tossed the plate in one of the pots by the fire. All he could do was hope the voices would quiet with time, even though a fearful worry in the back of his mind doubted it would happen.

6

ESCAPE

June, 904 A.D.
Paris, France

It didn't take long for Terric to realize his new master was building an army. What he couldn't figure out was why.

Only the soldiers were sent back to Ourea—the grunts and the obedient. Terric had to stay in the human realm, collecting new, moronic children for Niccoli. To date, they'd turned over eight hundred isen from various countries around Europe. Vikings, peasants, farmers—idiots, most of them.

Terric rarely wasted breath to speak to them, but they all called him Stone. He wore the name like armor until no one laughed anymore.

Although those around him left much to be desired,

at least Niccoli gave him plenty to read. And when he acquired too many books, Andor took them back to the guild with the new recruits.

Stone sat on a mattress in Paris, brushing the end of a quill pen on his nose as he paused to think. He stared out the window near his bed, eyes on the clock tower rising above the city. Eleven thirty. Andor would be back soon, and though he shared a room with the womanizing brute, Andor would often bring back books as he found them. Stone hoped the Viking had a new acquisition today, preferably something in French.

Someone whispered. Stone could barely make it out. His ear twitched, but he didn't look up. No one would be there. The bilingual souls he'd absorbed were chattier than Chad, but he could thankfully ignore them most of the time. Within seconds of stealing these souls, he knew French and Latin, science and alchemy, and so much more. Each soul brought him new insight in an instant.

He rubbed the quill on his nose again, savoring the tickle of the feather on his skin. As delightful as instant knowledge was, he'd made a terrible mistake.

Too late, he'd learned a precious truth—the more souls in an isen's mind, the more likely he would go mad. It was something Niccoli should have taught him, but the man made a poor mentor. His favorite phrase was "figure it out." And figure it out Stone had. He'd taught himself to control his barb after a month of shaming from his master. He'd uncovered a dozen languages through his soul acquisitions already, which unfortunately made him even more valuable as a translator. It was of no consequence; he would have done it anyway. To cheapen his brain out of resentment was a waste of his intellect. He could even pick up bits of a new language on his own now by listening to others speak.

But Stone couldn't make the same mistake. From now on, he would steal only what he needed to remain immortal: one soul every ten years.

Stone held his palm outright and summoned a flame into his hand. Simple. Easy. Niccoli had taught him how to do it after a few years, but not why it worked.

Why. He had to know *why*. His thirst for knowledge had been stymied all these years, blocked by the mundane hunt for more of the same unawaken isen, who all said the same dull things before Niccoli sent them to Death. But Ourea seemed to be the source of all the magic he'd found thus far, and Stone would never have his answer until he experienced this strange, new world for himself.

Eyes out of focus, he tapped on the window with his knuckle. Heads bobbed in the street below with nothing but the window separating him from them, yet he felt miles away. These humans would die soon, while he would live for centuries. Possibly forever if he could keep the voices in his head at bay. He had plans to fulfill, one of which included vengeance. He'd already begun building a fortune and intended to grow it over many generations. And once he had enough, he would buy the estate of his manor lord and burn it to the ground.

He smiled. That would be pleasant.

The church bell chimed twelve times. Noon. He paused, a half-finished sentence still taunting him in the open journal on his lap. He couldn't even remember what he'd been writing. Something about how he occasionally smelled something off around his fellow isen, but he couldn't place the scent. The words bunched together, tiny in his effort to conserve paper. His journal remained his one secret from Niccoli—the one thing his master didn't know he owned. He had to make it count.

He flipped through older entries, skimming his thoughts on the awakening process in an attempt to focus. He'd lost himself to thought a lot lately, often drifting into daydreams as he found himself less and less willing to put up with Niccoli's constant recruitment. The traveling, the brawls, the screams as Niccoli drowned his new children on their way to meet Death for the first time. Always the same—Niccoli would wait until the recruit awoke before sending them to Death, even if he didn't speak to them first.

Stone hated it. He saw himself in every panicked

attempt to hold onto life for a second longer. Little did they know they would come back—or that they would come back a slave.

He slammed the journal shut and grunted in frustration. That bastard. Niccoli made dying as painful as possible, and Stone couldn't figure out why. Based on his observations thus far, consciousness shouldn't be necessary to meet Death. Isen were born isen, but they didn't acquire their gifts until they met Death and came back. And if Stone were to prick an unawaken isen's neck before killing the person, he would become that isen's master. The newly awoken isen had to obey, always, as Stone had to obey Niccoli. But the why—that baffled him. It must have been a mental connection established when the spine was pricked before death, but the theory lacked substance.

To date, Stone hadn't figured out if other methods would work. Niccoli laughed at the idea and ignored Stone's suggestion to use stabbing or strangulation, saying only that something shouldn't be changed if it works. But Stone had to understand if other methods would work and if consciousness was key to its success.

He rubbed his face, recalling the frozen panic of drowning in the rock pool. He doubted his pain had been necessary, but he needed proof.

But… proof of what? That Niccoli was cruel? He'd proven that long ago.

The door swung open, and Stone shoved his journal under his blanket without looking up. He sat motionless, eyes focused on the wall opposite his bed, heart racing in the hope he'd been fast enough to hide his one secret.

Andor stomped into the room and left the door open behind him. In Stone's periphery, the Norseman cracked his neck and nodded in greeting.

Stone continued staring, willing the Viking to leave. He didn't like having to share a room, and he certainly didn't enjoy company even if it was with the isen he hated least. He'd been exploring isen awakening and delving into new understandings of isenhood. He didn't need interruptions.

Andor laughed and rubbed his beard. "Always a pleasure, Stone. It's good to see you haven't gotten kinder with age."

"Age means nothing to immortals," Stone said. He looked out the window. What a foolish Viking.

"It was a joke," the man said. The mattress squeaked from the weight of something, its metal frame groaning as more weight was added.

"I don't like jokes."

"Really?" Andor said, voice rising in pitch. Stone looked over, only to find Andor with a grin on his face, eyebrows raised.

Sarcasm. Oh.

"We're eating downstairs," Andor added, returning

to the bag now on the bed. He must have pulled it from under the mattress, but Andor's massive frame blocked whatever lay inside.

Stone didn't reply. He wondered why Andor would bother saying something so trivial. As much as he could appreciate science and the ideas in his books, he didn't understand his fellow isen or the humans they hunted. They wasted time on pleasantries and said things that didn't matter. It baffled him. Why waste the air?

"Are you coming?" Andor added after a moment.

An invitation. Oh.

"No." Stone pulled out *The Anglo-Saxon Chronicles* from under his bed and laid back, ready to read it for the ninety-seventh time.

Andor sighed and leaned on the wall with an open palm. "No, *thank you*. I appreciate the offer, Andor. You're a fine man, Andor. You've treated me well, Andor."

Stone grimaced and studied his roommate, wondering why he suddenly spoke in the third person. "Are you ill?"

Andor groaned and threw the bag under his bed. "You don't even try."

"Try to do what, exactly?"

"You do realize no one likes you, right?"

"I've been told, yes."

"And that doesn't bother you?"

Stone thought about it a moment and then shrugged. "Why would it? I find most people boring."

Andor stared at him a moment, cheek dented as if he were biting it. "Never mind. Enjoy your books."

The Viking stomped out of the room—every step like thunder, though he barely lifted his feet—and slammed the door behind him.

Stone eyed the door long after Andor left, wondering what had happened. He was inclined to think he'd made a mistake of some sort, but they'd simply been talking. All he'd done was turn down food and admit he was bored.

And he was—so very, very bored. Brutes and idiots, all of them. Except Andor. He seemed to be less of a brute and less of an idiot than the rest. But still.

Stone needed to break free, to escape Niccoli's control once and for all. He'd had enough. Five years of extended slavery with eternity to follow—he couldn't endure that. He couldn't take a second more of it.

He took a deep breath. He wouldn't. He wouldn't take any more of it.

He'd tried to escape before. Small attempts, like wandering to the back of a large group of new recruits in an effort to slip into the forest and disappear. He'd tried to sneak away while Niccoli turned a particularly strong isen who fought back. But both times, Niccoli had emerged ahead in the path a few minutes into the escape, always heading Stone off before he could truly run.

Perhaps, tonight would be different. With the overrun city full of people and a horde of isen spread throughout the mansion in which they'd taken residence, perhaps tonight would be in Stone's favor. Maybe he could lose himself in a crowd for once and truly slip away.

He jumped to his feet and grabbed his journal from beneath the blanket, tossing it into a bag that sat open on the floor. Several books followed, including his beloved *Anglo-Saxon Chronicles*. After throwing a hidden stash of dried beef, he tied the bag and slung it over his shoulder.

On the way to the door, he paused by the sword leaning against the wall. His sword, one Andor had given him. His decoration, the other isen called it, since he never used the thing. Although he did possess some basic knowledge due to some training from the Viking.

Stone tied the sheath around his waist and hoisted the bag over his shoulder once more. He slipped into a hallway covered in tapestries. Vivid thread outlined forests and mansions, with small, white beasts serving as horses. The hall stretched on either side of him, lined with dark wood and white walls. Gold sconces lit the air, casting orange light wherever daylight failed. The merchant who owned this home had welcomed Niccoli with a forced smile, and Stone didn't care to know their history. The man had wealth, and it served the isen well.

Conversations echoed from down the stairs to his right, followed by clinks of metal and mugs. He couldn't leave through the front door, of course, but he'd seen a second option. In his time at this merchant's house, he'd seen servants go in and out of a second staircase hidden behind a door at the end of the hall. He hurried over and pried it open, peeking into the darkness. An unlit stairwell stretched below him and opened onto a room below. He could only make out the first few feet of floorboards. No shadows passed by. No footsteps. No voices.

He took a deep breath and stole down the stairs, careful to keep one hand on the sword so that it didn't hit anything or make a sound.

Once at the bottom, he paused and peered into the room. A basin sat in one corner, full of brown water. Round and rectangular tables covered in towels and linens filled the rest of the room, some of them white but most of them covered in beige stains or red puddles. Only the barest of walkways cut through them. It seemed as though they'd been shoved here in a hurry, likely when Niccoli surprised his "dear friend," the merchant, with a visit.

Stone weighed his options. The dining room was at the front of the house, which meant he was unlikely to be seen out of the windows if he kept to the back and sides of the house. Many of the merchant's curtains remained drawn—likely to hide its visitors—but today, sun filled the room. He couldn't ignore the possibility other curtains had been opened as well. This staircase was at the rear of the house, and he suspected he would be able to go completely unseen if he could escape from here.

A glass window sat opposite the stairs. Stone hurried toward it and peeked outside. Sunshine. The street. People ambled by, and the occasional horse-drawn cart passed through the crowd. Conversation drifted through the glass. Someone cursed loud enough to make it through the window, and several men raced past. A short patch of grass separated the house from the road.

Freedom. Stone could lose himself in the crowd, and he would escape.

He unlocked the window and lifted it. In seconds, he'd slipped through. His feet landed on the grass, and a few sharp pains shot up his ankles. He grimaced but carried on.

The front of the house—and its sentries—were around the corner to his right. To his left—

One of the merchant's guards leaned against the face of a house to his left, which pressed against the merchant's home. The guard's eyes were closed, and Stone's heart skipped several beats. He charged into the crowd, not daring to close the window for fear of the guard hearing.

He crossed the street and slipped into an alley between two buildings. A woman shouted overhead, and liquid crashed into the path. The stink of waste and rotten meat assaulted his nose. He gagged and covered his mouth, suppressing vomit. Stone cringed and turned back toward the street, but the merchant's house stared at him from across the cobblestones. Its white face, faded in places, dared him to step out into the street again. Its windows watched him.

The alley it would be, then.

He held his breath and charged through the still-wet patch of the street, eyes on a road that appeared ahead past a few more houses.

He slipped into the crowd as it ambled along. A man glanced over as Stone entered the street, but it lasted barely a second. In moments, Stone was no longer worth examining. Nothing more than another peasant in the throng.

Stone smiled. The thrill of hope lit his chest. He wasn't free of Niccoli yet, but he was close. So close. He would be safest out of the city, and if he correctly recalled how they had entered, he needed to head north. Beyond that, he didn't care where he went as long as it was away from the isen he hated most.

Bodies surrounded him, and he took a deep breath to center himself in the masses. Sweat and urine wafted from the crowd like spoiled cologne. He wanted nothing more than to escape the throng and its stink, but he had to blend in. He kept his head down to avoid being seen. Men walked past, some accompanied by women, and the occasional cart split the crowd.

Another man walked up beside him and kept pace. Stone turned his head away, enough to hide most of his face, but the stranger didn't move past him. He matched Stone's gait.

"Are you enjoying your stroll?" Niccoli asked. *Yor strohll.*

Stone let out a long breath and stopped midstride. The crowd parted. One man smacked his shoulder. Several voices complained as he stood in the middle of the road, redirecting a flood of people around him.

"Ecartez-vous!"

"Bougez-vous, imbécile!"

The crowds flowed around him, frowning and shaking fists in his periphery. He didn't care. Niccoli pulled ahead and stopped, his familiar dark hair and pale skin like an anchor tearing through Stone's hope. The isen master waited, hands in his pockets as he smirked.

Sweat pooled along Stone's hairline. "How do you always know where I am?"

"I own you, boy," Niccoli said with a shrug.

"I only want to explore. Discover. Learn. Yet—"

"What you want doesn't matter. Someday, I won't need you anymore, and you'll be free to do as you please. For now, you stay and obey. Shall we?" He gestured to an alley to Stone's right. Past the bobbing heads of the next street over, the white merchant house glimmered in the sun.

Stone hung his head but nodded. It had been a request, certainly, but he couldn't run. He couldn't escape, not with Niccoli so near. He'd be commanded back, and it would only anger his master. The man would get revenge in some petty way later if Stone didn't obey now.

He plodded down the alley, not bothering to cover his nose as the stench of waste overpowered him.

If it was the last thing Stone did, he would break the bond with Niccoli. He hadn't faced Death itself to be an eternal slave.

7

THEFT

June, 904 A.D.
Paris, France

"Why are we here, Niccoli?" Stone asked.

He sat on the slanted roof of a Parisian house, far enough back to hide from any prying eyes on the fairly empty street below. They'd slipped into a wealthy district with service entrances and little foot traffic. Paris stretched out before him, nothing but roofs. Two days had passed since his attempted escape, but to date, he'd suffered no retribution or punishment. Yet.

His master had led him up to the Parisian roof with nothing but a gesture and the word, "Come." No explanation. No reasoning. Only a silent ten-minute walk through the streets and an agonizing three-story climb up the side of a stone house.

Niccoli clicked his tongue in disappointment. "You must make your first child. Most isen have begun their families by now. You apparently need prodding."

Stone grimaced. He didn't want to doom another life to Niccoli's guild. Besides, Stone often heard he was intolerable. Any isen he turned would probably hate him and Niccoli equally.

Instead of raising either point, he gestured to the open sky. "I fail to see how I can do that while on a roof."

"Look in the garden."

Stone obeyed. Across the street, he noticed a white building with blue shutters. A fence separated it and a garden from the road. The houses on either side had similar yards, nothing on any property touching another save for the fences.

A young woman of, perhaps, fifteen sat on a stool in the garden, her legs tucked to her side as she read a beige book. Her black hair was tied in a bun at the base of her neck, and a blue dress spilled around her. Her skin paled in the sunlight, as if it couldn't take the heat, and she wiped a small hand across her brow.

"The girl?" Stone asked.

Niccoli nodded. "She has the isen gift, though it skipped her father."

"It skips generations?"

"Often. Sometimes two. But it always reappears."

"How can you tell she's one of us?"

"She has the isen scent."

Stone paused and scrunched his eyebrows together. "And what's that?"

"It's our perfume of sorts. Our scent. It's subtle in unawaken isen, but there all the same. A mix of lilac and pine. Can't you smell it?"

Stone took a deep breath, and he detected a hint of pine mixed with a floral undertone wafting from Niccoli. Perhaps that was the odd scent he caught off his fellow isen now and then.

"What if that's all it is—perfume? She seems wealthy enough to have such a thing."

"No perfume contains the powerful sway of the isen scent. Few know this, but it can alter emotion and captivate our prey. No, she has the gift."

Stone recalled the scent radiating from Niccoli all those years ago, on the day he was turned. He hadn't understood his fear then, but it made sense. He'd been targeted, captivated by the stranger in his village. The alarming scent had been a warning he hadn't heeded.

"Prick her spine and make her yours," Niccoli ordered.

The pull of a command tugged on Stone's gut. He cringed. He would have to obey this order. And he didn't want to know if Niccoli had meant more than simply turning her. Stone had never made any woman his and didn't intend to start now.

"Give me time," Stone said.

"You have three days." Niccoli stood and climbed over the roof to the corner they'd climbed.

Stone groaned and rubbed his face. Fine. He hated his master, but he could at least appreciate the man's brevity. In three days, this woman would have a new life, whether she wanted it or—as was more likely—not.

S tone watched the woman's house for two days from the roof across the street. No one seemed to notice him, but he was careful to keep out of view of the roadway. He didn't need unwelcome attention.

The house's front gates opened onto the street, and an alley ran behind it, separating the home from its equally wealthy neighbors. After a day of observation, he discovered her bedroom to be on the second floor, in the back of the house. Several other bedrooms flanked it, so getting to her would be difficult. Luckily, only she, her mother, and her father lived in the house with their servants.

Despite the summer sunshine, the girl sat in a downstairs window today, her nose pointed once more to a book. She held a new one this morning with a cover as black as her hair.

She rarely walked outside, seeming to prefer the window to the garden. And for two days, she did nothing but read.

Amidst the sweat and sunburn of sitting so long on a roof, Stone had an idea. Death must have known more than he'd let on, and this girl would visit him soon. Since she could read, perhaps she had the where-withal to memorize a few questions for the specter. Stone tapped his cheek in thought. If he could ask Death anything, what would it be?

Movement in his periphery caught his attention. A man stood at the window, and the girl turned to him without setting down her book. He pointed a finger in her face, and she leaned away. They exchanged words. He knocked the book out of her hand. It fell to the floor. She stood, but the man slapped her. Her knees buckled. She fell to the window seat, shoulders trem-bling as she sobbed. The man disappeared into the house, out of sight.

Her father, perhaps. Stone rubbed his neck, wondering if any isen he turned in the future would simply trade one life of slavery for another, much like him.

Stone had a plan, but it required a finesse he wasn't sure he possessed. He needed rope, poison hemlock, opium, and the key to the manor. Thus far, he'd secured most of them either through theft or borrowing. Andor already had rope under his bed— Stone had checked—and now there were only two more items to acquire.

He patted the stolen key in his pocket, satisfied with his quick fingers and the unsuspecting servant who'd left for the food market. She hadn't even noticed him lift it from her. When she returned without it, Stone imagined she would avoid sharing the fact she'd lost such an important item and instead retrace her steps, giving him at least one night to sneak inside the house. It was all he needed.

He walked through the busy streets of a specialty market, searching for a medicine shop he'd found the previous day. Its faded sign hung above a closed door, and he headed for it, a few extra coins than usual jingling in his pocket. One of his previous conquests had been a rich, French bachelor with as many coins as books, and luckily Stone had escaped the house with most of both.

The door creaked as Stone pushed it open. A shopkeeper stood in the middle of a room barely six feet wide. Bottles filled shelves along the walls, and those shelves covered most of the free space. Most bottles were brown, but a few blue and red ones caught Stone's eye. The shopkeeper's gray hair receded along his temples and the top of his head. A few silver strands poked from his ears.

"I need a sleep aid," Stone said in French.

The French shopkeeper nodded, as if he'd heard it all before, and answered in French. "The wife has trouble sleeping?"

Stone nodded instead of speaking. He hadn't improved as a liar since his days with the manor lord, and he doubted the shopkeeper believed the lie. He still looked seventeen, and that was young for most men to marry.

"I recommend the dream elixir." The shopkeeper reached for a brown bottle with a cloud painted in black ink on a beige label.

"What's in it?"

The man smiled. "No one asks that. Are you an apprentice to an alchemist?"

"Yes," Stone lied.

The shopkeeper tapped the glass. "It's made of mandragora bark, hyoscyamus seed, and extract of opium, so it comes at a quite a price."

Stone waved the thought away. "It will do. But my wife can barely sleep, and I would like a bottle of opium as well."

The shopkeeper nodded and lifted a second, square

bottle, barely three fingers wide. "I have that as well. I assume you know how to use—"

Stone nodded. The brown bottle would put her under in seconds, while a small sip of the opium would keep her asleep while he transported her. The rest of the opium bottle, mixed with the poison hemlock he'd secured from another shopkeeper earlier, would kill her.

The man lifted the brown bottle he'd first suggested. "For this, a few drops on a rag under the nose before bed will be enough, so the bottle will last quite a while."

Stone nodded, but he intended to use half the bottle. He was going to kill the girl, after all. Dosage didn't matter.

Night fell too slowly for Stone's taste, but a crescent moon finally rose over Paris. He crept into the alley behind the girl's house and waited. Candlelight flickered in an upstairs bedroom, casting the girl's shadow along the wall by the window. He groaned. Only she would stay up past dark, likely to read.

He kept to the shadows, losing himself in thought as he waited for her to sleep. He'd already decided: if he had to kill and awaken her as an isen, he would at least experiment with it. Instead of drowning her, he would use his opium and poison hemlock concoction. It would put her painlessly to death and, more importantly, save her the pain he'd endured.

Truth be told, he was doing a shoddy job of experimentation. Only one factor should change at a time, but he didn't have access to water worth drowning someone in, and he didn't intend to see her life fade from her eyes as he killed her.

The candlelight popped out of existence, and darkness consumed her room.

Stone squared his shoulders and took a breath, hardly believing he could do this. He crept from the alley to a door in the back of the house and pulled the stolen key from his pocket. Metal clinked as he inserted the key, and the latch clicked open. He smirked at his non-magical solution.

He eased the handle down and, as slowly as he could, pushed the door open. A dark room greeted him with stairs to his right and another door ahead to the left. Brooms filled one corner, while buckets of water with rags hanging over them littered one side of the floor. The dim glow of blue moonlight spilled in from behind him, casting his shadow on the buckets.

He set the key on the floor, as he no longer needed it, and crept up the stairwell, careful to walk along the edges to avoid creaks. The wood groaned beneath his weight on occasion as he took the dark stairs with careful steps.

The staircase ended at a closed door. He pressed his ear to the wood and listened. The grains scratched his ear, rough and old, but he heard nothing on the other side.

He took a deep breath. He could do this. He had to.

The door slid open without a sound, and he stepped into the hall. Her room would be to the left and against the back of the house. He hurried past the closed doors toward her.

When he reached the last door on the left, he leaned into the handle and opened the door without a sound. Moonlight poured into her bedroom through open curtains, illuminating a lump in a four-poster bed against the far wall. Aside from that, a chest sat against the wall to his left and tapestries covered the walls, though he couldn't make out their designs in the darkness.

She lay in the bed, her back to him. Her black hair covered her pillow in thick curls. Her thin form barely lifted the blanket with each breath. Up close, Stone could finally detect the isen scent Niccoli had mentioned. Lilac and pine spun in the air, tickling his lungs until a sneeze threatened him. He pinched his nose, quelling the impulse.

Her blanket hung over the side of the mattress. He pulled the bottle from his pocket and gathered a bit of her blanket in his hand. Eyes on hers to ensure she didn't wake, he poured half the bottle onto the comforter and held it to her mouth before he could question himself.

She flinched. Her eyelids shot open, and her black eyes widened as she saw him. They captivated him for a second, their darkness a sharp contrast to the dim glow of the moon. But her small hand grabbed his wrist, shaking him from his thoughts. She wrestled with him and twisted her head away from the cloth, so he set down the bottle and held her head in place. She shouted, her voice muffled by the fabric, and Stone wished he'd closed her door all the way. But no one came, and in a few moments, her eyes rolled back in her head. She stilled beneath him.

He let out a shaky breath and opened her mouth with one hand. From his pocket, he pulled out a small bottle with barely any opium in it. He'd emptied the rest into his poison hemlock concoction, which rested on the windowsill back in his room. This small dose of the leftovers would keep her asleep until he could transport her there—at least, he hoped as much.

Stone poured the spoonful's worth of pure opium into her mouth, closed her lips, held her nose, and waited for her to swallow out of instinct. She obliged him with a gurgle.

Good. That would keep her asleep while he trudged back to his host's home. Now for the hard part.

He knelt and pulled her into his arms, but she weighed on what few muscles he had despite her petite form. Knees shaking, he grunted and slung her over his shoulder with the silent hope he could keep from dropping her on the trek back to the merchant's home. Picking her up off the ground would be torment.

Footsteps echoed in the hall. A pang of dread rocked his core like a wave of ice through his veins. Stone gulped. He crossed to the wall and peered out of the crack in the door.

A man appeared, walking up the steps to the left of the hall. But as he cleared the stairs, he turned instead toward the still-open servant's door.

Stone held his breath. The man stopped by it and set his hands on his waist. He shook his head and swung the door closed. It slammed. Stone flinched. The girl slipped on his shoulder, and he grunted as he adjusted her back into place.

The man cursed and retreated to a door at the far end of the hall and entered, slamming it with the same force once he was through.

Stone nudged the door open and crept back to the servant's staircase. The girl slowed his route. At this rate, her weight would double his ten-minute trip to the merchant house. He would have to stay in the shadows to avoid patrols, and he hadn't taken into account how quickly holding her would tire his arms. Still, he would find a way to get her back to the merchant's house. He had to. And he would likely curse Niccoli the entire way.

Thirty minutes later, Stone kicked open the door to his shared bedroom, no longer caring about keeping silent now that he'd finally made it to the blasted merchant's house.

His arms and shoulders screamed for mercy under the tiny woman's weight, and his knees threatened to give out on him at any moment. He could hardly believe he'd made it without dropping her. Well, she had slipped at one point, and her head smacked against a brick wall, but she wasn't bleeding. She would be fine.

He unloaded her onto his bed and fell to his knees, sucking in air as he tried to regain his composure. Blasted Niccoli. Stupid isen. Idiot commands. He could be in bed right now, or better yet, reading a new book instead of wasting his money on a sleeping aid and opium.

Andor snored from the other bed, and Stone smacked his fist against his own mattress in annoyance. Never a moment's peace.

Stone pushed himself to his feet and retrieved the rope from under Andor's bed. The bloody Viking didn't even flinch. Some warrior.

The rope scratched his fingers, but he set to work. He wrapped it around the girl's torso and legs in an effort to keep her still. He didn't need her running off once she woke up, as he had questions to ask her and poison for her to take.

With a groan and a deep breath, he hoped his plan would work.

He grabbed his journal and quill. Resting it on his thigh, he scratched his questions to Death in French on a blank sheet of parchment, leaving ample space for Death's answers once—if—she returned.

How does magic work?

How does an isen break the bond with his master?

What is a soul?

That done, he set the journal on the windowsill and crossed the room to the white, wash basin sitting by the window. Hands cupped, he dipped his hands into the water basin. The liquid cooled his hands, and he could finally breathe a little easier. Careful not to trip, he carried the water to his bed and dumped it on her face.

She sputtered and coughed, squeezing her eyes as the water woke her. Her eyes opened, but she couldn't seem to focus them. Her head rolled to one side, no doubt still affected by the opium. Still, she struggled against the rope, eyes flitting to Stone every now and then as she fought her restraints.

"What—help! Who are you?" she asked in French, voice a bit slurred.

Stone answered in her language. "Hush. You're fine. I'm sending you to meet an old friend of mine. Read these." Stone held the journal open to her face.

She answered in English. "What's that? Let me go! Curse you, English idiot."

He smirked. She must have placed his accent. She was smarter than he thought. He nodded. "I am English, yes, and very well may be an idiot for doing this. But I need you to ask my friend these questions."

"Never. Do you know who I am? Release me and tell me this minute what's happening!"

"I'll explain everything as soon as you recite these questions from memory."

Her eyes flitted to the page, and she cursed under her breath. "Magic? What is—"

Stone lowered his journal. "Recite them back to me."

She struggled against the rope, but Stone smacked her shoulder. She flinched, frowning, and recited his questions back to him.

"Lovely job," he said with a nod.

"Now, release me!"

"Soon." There were a few matters he needed to tend to first.

Stone grabbed the sleeping aid from his pocket and emptied its contents on his blanket. She shouted for help, but he smothered her once more with the blanket until her eyes closed and she was still.

His journal had been kicked to the floor in the scuffle, and he ran a hand through his hair as he pulled it closer. Exhaustion tugged on his eyes, but he couldn't sleep. Not yet.

He flipped back a few pages to his notes on awakening an isen, taken from years of watching Niccoli kill his new recruits. One sketch showed the exact placement of where to put the barb in her neck, and Stone swallowed hard. Now or never.

The rope tickled his hands as he reached to untie her. She shifted a bit with each of his tugs at the ropes but didn't stir. It took a few seconds to free her, but he finally lifted her onto her side. She rolled without resistance. The barb slid out of his palm, and he placed it below the bone at the base of her neck. He pushed. It slipped into her skin. A jolt flew up his arm—almost pain, but mostly shock. Disgust. A little fear.

She choked, gurgling, but the purple thorn slid in without an issue.

His body began operating on its own as he fought to ignore the sensation of pricking another isen. It had shaken him to his core, and yet he couldn't bring himself to study the sensation. Not yet.

He retracted the barb as quickly as he'd pierced her neck and laid her on her back. He re-tied the ropes, arms moving without conscious thought on his part.

He tried not to think about what would come next, but it consumed him as he went through the motions of preparing to kill her.

Stone lifted the opium and poison hemlock concoction from its place on the windowsill and paused to prepare himself. He pinched her mouth open. Her eyes still closed, she didn't resist. He emptied the small bottle into her mouth and closed her jaw. A dribble of liquid leaked from the corners of her mouth. He pinched her nose and held her jaw closed. She choked once and swallowed.

The concoction would take minutes to work, and she would feel nothing. No pain. No fear. Only sleep. He envied that—if it worked.

Hands over his mouth, Stone closed his eyes and listened for her breath, willing it to end. He counted the seconds and then minutes as they crept by. Finally, her breathing slowed. She wheezed, each breath grating like nails across a rock. In seconds, her chest stopped moving entirely. Andor's snoring, louder now than before, replaced her gasping.

Stone backed away and tripped on her knee, falling to the floor with a thud. He backed against the wall, eyes on her as he covered his mouth with a hand. He could barely get enough breath to keep from fainting but shoving his back against the wall to brace himself seemed to help. He could barely process what was happening as he fought to slow his racing heart.

He hoped this worked. He'd done everything exactly as Niccoli had done it, short of causing her pain. He didn't know how long she would be out. It varied from isen to isen, and he had nothing concrete to go on. He examined the clock tower out of his window, but a silhouette greeted him. The moonlight didn't illuminate its face, so Stone had no idea of the time. He listened for an hour's chime, but the night gave him nothing.

He would have to time with the next one, if he ever turned another isen. As it stood, he'd had enough of the whole ordeal to last him a lifetime.

Exhaustion tugged on his eyelids, and he longed to close them. But, tired as he was, Stone wouldn't sleep. He couldn't make a mistake, or he might finally feel the wrath Niccoli seemed to hide beneath the surface of his calm appearance. He had to simply wait with the hope she would awake.

8

AWAKENING

June, 904 A.D.
Paris, France

Stone awoke to a muffled curse and the thunk of an elbow smacking wood.

He jolted awake, eyes blurry from sleep. Two silhouettes wrestled in front of the window, one three times the size of the other. He rubbed his eyes, only to see the girl struggling with Andor. The Viking's massive arms wrapped around her, but she wriggled with all the desperation of a snake backed into a corner.

The ropes he'd used to bind her lay on the floor beside the bed. She'd escaped. At least she wasn't one to play the victim. Stone could appreciate that.

Her eyes shifted to him. She gasped and bit Andor's wrist, as if suddenly even more desperate to get away.

Andor cursed in a language Stone still hadn't learned and shook his hand, but his other arm still wound around her shoulders to keep her in place. She kicked and scratched at him, but the great Viking laughed.

"This one's feisty!" Andor shouted.

"Enough of this. Stop it," Stone snapped, eyes on the girl.

She didn't. She scratched and fought harder than before, legs flailing as she struggled to get free.

A twinge of annoyance pulsed in Stone's temple. He tried again, this time borrowing the tone Niccoli used any time he issued an order Stone couldn't disobey. "Stop at once!"

The girl flinched and stood still as a statue, eyes wide and focused now on Stone. Her jaw dropped open, and her hands fell to her sides.

Andor nodded and released her, stomping back to his bed with the strides of an elephant. Stone resisted the impulse to groan.

"How did you do that?" the girl asked.

He paused, wondering where to start. Introductions, probably. "I'm Stone."

She pursed her lips and paused, eyeing him for a moment. "My name is Vivienne Baudin, daughter of—"

"I don't care." Stone waved away her formalities with a flick of his wrist.

She bristled. "Rude!"

"You don't even know, child," Andor said under his breath. He bit into a green apple and smiled as Stone caught his eye.

"Leave," Stone said with a nod to the door.

Andor's grin widened. "Not a chance! Watching you stumble along with your first child is far too entertaining."

"Child? What?" Vivienne asked.

"Andor, give me ten minutes alone," Stone insisted.

"Not happening. Your little miss almost escaped, and she's only here thanks to me. I've earned my seat, and—"

"Please, Andor."

The Viking's eyebrows shot into the loose hair hanging around his face, and for a moment, the man didn't seem able to speak.

"Ten minutes," he eventually mumbled. He lumbered toward the door and slammed it behind him, though his footsteps thumped along the hall for several seconds before the room once more became silent.

Stone examined his acquisition, the girl named Vivienne, and wondered where to begin. She studied him, back arched and chin high, but her knees shook. Fear. Pride. Neither would serve her in the isen ranks.

He sighed. "You and I are isen, girl, and I have quite a lot to tell you."

⁂

"I had no idea I was an… isen, you called it?"

Stone nodded in answer to Vivienne's question, grateful to no longer be speaking. He'd explained her new life for about thirty minutes, far exceeding the ten he'd been given, but luckily Andor hadn't returned.

Vivienne wrung her hands. Stone didn't know how well he'd explained everything, but she seemed to understand most of it.

"Did you feel any pain?" he asked.

She shook her head. Good. He sat a little straighter, content that his experiment had worked.

Vivienne bit her lip. "You controlled me, then, when you told me to stop struggling with that brute."

Stone smirked but nodded again. "To the best of my ability, I will not control you unless you do something stupid. I don't particularly enjoy it."

"My father would love to be able to control me like that," she said with a glare out the window.

Oh, right. Stone forgot this particular detail. "You can't go back to him."

She curled her knees beneath her chin and wrapped her arms around her shins. "I don't mind. All I'll miss are my books."

Stone paused, watching her stare out the window. Finally. Finally, one other person in his life could respect and understand the knowledge he craved.

He reached into the bag beside his bed and shook loose a French tome, something Andor had brought in a few weeks ago. He handed it to her. "We have plenty."

A thin smile erupted on her face. Her cheeks regained some of their color, and her eyes lit up with something Stone didn't recognize—gratitude, maybe? She wrapped her slender fingers around its binding. "Thank you. That's kind."

Stone shook his head. "I've read it twice. I was going to send it back with Andor, but you might as well have a look through it first."

Her smile didn't fade, which surprised him. Usually if someone smiled at him, it only took a few words out of his mouth to wipe it away. He didn't understand why—it simply happened.

"Now, about my questions for Death," Stone began.

She laughed. "I'm grateful at least he could explain what was happening. I was terrified, and you were useless."

"I often am. But did you ask—"

She waved away his thought. "Yes, yes, I asked him. But you won't like the answers."

Stone sat straighter. "I don't care. Tell me."

She pursed her lips again. "His answer was 'everything is energy.'"

Stone paused. "To which question?"

"All of them." She smirked.

Stone stood and backed toward the window, watching her. He frowned and rubbed his chin. "That's absolutely useless."

She shrugged. "It's all he would tell me. He actually laughed when I asked. What a peculiar sound. Like—"

"Are you hungry?" Stone asked without looking at her.

"A bit, yes. What—"

"I'll return in a moment. Don't leave." He didn't command her. He didn't need to, as she had a book to keep her busy. With that, he exited into the hall and shut the door behind him. She said something, her voice muffled through the door, and he made out a curse in her words.

How aggravating. Death had once again tricked him by wasting an opportunity for answers. He had to distract himself, to piece together any clues lingering in the vague reply, so he headed for the kitchens to find food for his new conquest.

But as he walked down the hallway, something pulsed in his chest. It was as if a beacon of energy burned in the back of his mind, growing more and more distant as he walked away from his room. He'd never encountered this before, or—

Stone paused and spun around, eyes on his door. The beacon pointed to *her*.

His jaw dropped. The beacon told him where his child isen was, even through walls and tapestries. It all made sense. No wonder Niccoli always knew where Stone went. All Niccoli had to do was look for the beacon in a place where it shouldn't be.

Stone rubbed his jaw in defeat and leaned against a wall, a weight pressing on his shoulders. He could never escape Niccoli, not unless—

He snapped to attention, thoughts racing through his mind as he pieced together possibilities. Not unless Niccoli was distracted, or if perhaps multiple children diluted the power of the beacon. With so many isen children in his horde, Niccoli must have had trouble keeping tabs on them all. Perhaps he'd come to expect Stone to run, and thus paid more attention to him. But if Stone could somehow convince Niccoli to focus on someone else, lure him into a false sense of security…

Stone tapped his finger on his chin, deep in thought, and continued walking without paying attention to the manor around him.

He could turn more isen to test whether or not that could dilute the power of the beacon, but he doubted he had the stomach for it. He'd hated turning even Vivienne, and he didn't think he could do it again. Not for quite some time, at least. He did, however, learn that the turn didn't have to be painful. Vivienne hadn't felt a thing. Niccoli was merely cruel for making his children awaken before their deaths.

Stone found the stairs and began down them, only to see Niccoli emerge from a room nearby. Stone paused and straightened. Niccoli smiled, his eyes creasing, but Stone knew better.

Niccoli only smiled when he was about to strike.

"Stone, how good to see you." *Stohne.*

Stone skipped the formalities. "It was a success. She's an isen now."

"I know."

"How?"

Niccoli grinned but ignored the question. "I would like to go home for a while. We've all made such progress in Paris, and we have earned a break."

"Home?"

"Ourea, my boy. To the guild. We leave tonight. Pack your things." He patted Stone on the shoulder and passed him on the stairs.

A sliver of excitement swam in Stone's gut. Perhaps this was what others felt when in love, or whatever foolish emotions they had on a daily basis. Despite Death's terrible answers and the discovery of his new beacon, Stone grinned.

Ourea. *Finally.*

9
OUREA

S tone adjusted the sword around his waist—his decoration, as so many often reminded him—and scanned the forest. His pack weighed on his shoulders, heavy with his books, ink, quills, and precious journal.

He and his fellow isen had walked for hours in the night and now lumbered through the forests outside Paris. He couldn't name where they'd gone, or the road they'd taken, despite keeping a watchful eye for possible chances to escape. Nothing but a habit, really, at this point. Now that he understood Niccoli could sense his every move, a flurry of frustration burned in his chest at the thought of escape.

Vivienne marched alongside him, keeping close to his side in the herd of isen. Fifteen of Niccoli's children surrounded them, all new recruits who had never seen Ourea except for Andor. The Viking led the way, apparently familiar with this route. Niccoli kept to the rear, presumably to encourage stragglers along.

Twigs crunched beneath Stone's feet as he continued through the forest without a path. The moon that had illuminated his escape from Vivienne's home no longer helped them here, as the moonlight couldn't break through the summer canopy. How Andor knew the way was beyond Stone. As far as he could tell, no landmarks served to guide them toward the lichgate that would take them to Ourea.

He grinned. He'd heard about these things and couldn't wait to see one. Lichgates were portals into another world and full of magic for him to dissect.

Andor stopped between two trees and beckoned the group closer. Two branches—one from each tree—crossed overhead, making an arch of sorts. A silver gleam illuminated the woods through the trees, and Stone paused to process what he was seeing.

Moonlight. Despite the thick forest blocking the moon overhead, the space between the trees gleamed with a white glow. A path cut through ferns and bushes, the dirt almost dark blue in the night. Greenery littered the underbrush, thick and still but muted, as if a paper-thin cloth hung between the trees and moved with each breath of the wind.

A hand clasped Stone's shoulder, and he flinched. Niccoli appeared beside him, quiet enough that Stone hadn't heard the crunch of his boots on the forest floor.

His master laughed. "Nervous?"

Stone shook his head but didn't answer.

"Welcome to Ourea," Niccoli said.

He walked ahead and passed through the two trees, and once on the other side, his skin paled. He seemed a world away, as if in a painting. He looked around and walked to the left, and after he passed the trunk, he disappeared from sight.

Without warning, a pang of doubt hit Stone in the chest.

The hope he'd allowed himself thus far failed him. If his history with Niccoli told him anything, this had to be a ruse. All logic—everything Stone understood—told him Niccoli would appear on the other side of the tree. Perhaps his master had played an elaborate trick, and this would be the moment Stone learned the truth. Magic portals shouldn't exist, and if they didn't, Ourea couldn't exist, either. He would yet again be played for a fool. He braced himself, waiting for his mentor to appear around the tree, laughing at the great joke he'd played on them all.

But Niccoli didn't reappear. He couldn't hide behind the tree for long; it wasn't wide enough. No—

after walking through the portal, Niccoli had, in fact, disappeared.

Stone sucked in a breath of air, thrilled.

Andor followed, and several isen whose names Stone didn't care to learn followed suit. One after another, they funneled through. Several held their stomachs for a moment after entering, but they seemed to recover quickly enough and marched on, following Andor.

Stone studied the tree to his right as his fellow isen passed through. The tree itself wasn't special—bark, branches, grime. A tree. But the portal beside it—Stone smiled. The air hummed, vibrating in a thin sheet connecting the two trees. It shifted, ceaseless, like water. He couldn't focus on it. His eyes stung and blurred until he gave up and stepped back, admiring it from afar.

Vivienne tapped his shoulder.

"Hmm?" he asked, not bothering to look over.

"Are we going, too?"

Stone blinked and snapped out of his thoughts. They stood alone in the forest, as apparently the rest of the isen had already gone through. Niccoli stood on the other side, eyebrow twisted in either annoyance or curiosity. Stone couldn't tell which.

He cleared his throat. "Yes, after you. Go."

Vivienne stepped through and doubled over, one

hand on her stomach. She set her free hand against a tree on the other side and leaned onto it.

Interesting reaction. Stone made a mental note and stepped through as well.

A flash of blue light in his peripheral vision blinded him, and pain ripped through his stomach as if someone had kicked him in the gut. His cheeks flushed with nausea. He bent, hands on his knees, and gasped through several breaths before he could properly breathe again. Vivienne cursed, but Stone remained silent. He waited for the nausea to pass. As the bile receded from his throat, he stood and adjusted his shirt, composing himself.

"Come, come. It's not that bad," Niccoli said.

Twigs snapped, and Stone's ear twitched at the sound. He opened his eyes and studied the ground. Purple leaves covered the forest floor, sprinkled with twigs that wove around each other. Silver light illuminated them. He looked up, and sure enough, a full moon peeked through gaps in the canopy.

"Hurry," Vivienne said under her breath.

Stone looked down and found Vivienne tugging on his sleeve. Niccoli stood not far off, eyes narrowed and focused on him.

Ugh. Not a moment to study this wondrous new world. Not one. Stone clenched his fist, tempted to speak his mind, but held his tongue. He knew better.

Instead, he nodded and followed his master, ever the begrudgingly, obedient boy.

Something in the branches above shrieked. It was the screech of a woman in agony, and the pitch reminded Stone of a fox's cry if it were held underwater. The creatures had startled him once too often in his travels, shouting to their neighbors as he wondered if a woman lay dying in the woods. But they would always scamper off, and the screech would stop. He waited for the telltale skittering of feet through the underbrush, but it never came.

Vivienne grabbed Stone's arm, her body closer than ever before, and Stone allowed it. The sound fascinated him. He couldn't think of a creature that could make such a noise and live in a tree, so he longed to see it.

"What was that?" Stone asked.

Niccoli continued without answering. Stone frowned but followed. More screams filled the forest, some quieter than others. Birds twittered. The underbrush rustled. This forest was alive, full of creatures Stone may never see again, and he had to trudge along behind his master. His frown deepened to a scowl, and tension pulled on his shoulders. He longed to strangle Niccoli or shove his sword through the man's eye. Only a violent end would suit such a terrible person. And at the second death, Niccoli wouldn't be allowed to return to Earth.

Ahead, Andor stepped through a thick wall of vines.

They parted as if someone held them open for him, and daylight spilled past the leaves. The group passed through, light illuminating each face as he or she entered.

Yet again, Stone passed through last, only to realize that the light came from yet another lichgate. Two trees stood within the wall of vines, lichen hanging from their branches. Two of these branches crossed, creating an arch between the two trees similar to the first lichgate they'd seen. Through this portal, finches dove along the waves of a lake, which sparkled in the daylight. Across the glittering surface, mountains blocked the horizon

"Not another one," Vivienne mumbled under her breath.

"How is it day in there?" he asked no one in particular.

Though no one answered, he could guess. Each portal must take them to another part of Ourea, which would mean while it was night where they were now, it was midday in another part of the world. They could hop from place to place, thousands of miles away from the first location, in seconds.

Stone grinned. Marvelous.

The last of the isen group passed through, and Niccoli stood to the side, waiting. He gestured for Stone to enter. Stone obliged, and once more the blue light preceded a kick to the gut from some unknown force. He doubled over again on the grass, hands on his knees, and suppressed the desire to vomit. In his peripheral vision, several other isen knelt in a similar fashion.

He spun, anxious to see what the lichgate looked like from the other side. Two trees anchored in the mud of the bank, their branches crossed in a gate so similar to the first two. Nothing hid the portal. It simply protruded from the sand like a doorway to the night.

His shoulders fell. How obvious.

Beyond the lichgate, the mud became brown grass. Past that, a wall of trees stretched as far as Stone could see. A dirt path wove alongside them, and many of the isen had already begun along it. He followed.

Within moments, the woods choked the path and forced everyone into single-file. The trunks huddled close together, too close to walk in between. Grass began to break through the soil in their road. Vines crept along the trees, strangling the trunks.

A floral perfume broke the monotony of their walk, and Stone welcomed the distraction. He tried to place the scent, and it came to him within seconds.

Lilac.

Around a bend in the road, a clearing broke into the path and allowed more space to spread out. Grass covered what remained of the trail, and though it continued ahead, Andor veered into the new space.

Closely knit trees and a rim of lilac bushes framed the circle. The purple flowers offered a stark contrast to the pale brown of the forest wood.

A doorway had been cut into the trees, and the herd of isen funneled toward it. Together, they crossed the purple threshold. The heat of the sun dissolved, leaving only the cool chill of a shaded wood with no breeze. Sunbeams broke through the leaves here and there, filling the path with a yellow-green glow.

Stone glanced upward. A man sat on a branch stemming from the second tree along the path. He wore a hooded shirt that covered much of his pale face. The man frowned, the lines in his forehead deepening as Stone caught his eye.

The path widened, about twenty feet now, and the isen around Stone spread out as the last of the natural light dissolved. Trees on either side of them stretched at least two stories high, creating a tunnel of branches that blocked out the sun. Metal cages hung from the limbs along the center, each holding a thick candle that spread enough light to illuminate the walkway. Shadows flickered across the trunks on either side of the path, but Stone didn't pay them any mind. They seemed to bother Vivienne, for whatever reason. She tensed her jaw and stayed close.

The road twisted and turned for a good ten minutes, until a pale light appeared around a bend. Stone blinked, eyes already unaccustomed to sunlight.

When his vision adjusted, a rocky mansion came into focus. It filled the center of a massive clearing wider than anything he'd seen in his life—at least the size of the grazing fields in the manor where he'd grown up. The house itself stretched five or six stories tall, with at least two dozen widows facing him on each floor. The roof sloped in a violent arch, its shingles beige in the sunlight.

The sun blazed through an opening in the canopy, its beams illuminating the ground with a yellow glow, but the heat didn't reach Stone. He waited for the next order, curious as to what would come next.

Several smaller houses dotted the edge of the clearing, about half the size of the great mansion in the middle. Dirt paths connected the various houses. People filled the space, walking from the mansion or shaking sheets out of windows, and most wore the same beige pants. Other walkways, similar to the entrance, cut through the forest around the house, no doubt pathways to other clearings like this one. Stone wondered how deep the labyrinth went.

He took a step back, a tad disgusted by the sheer number of people. "How many isen children do you have, Niccoli?"

His master shook his head. "Not enough. Most here are slaves, used for farming and cleaning. Some are for reproduction as well, though not many produce isen for me."

Stone gritted his teeth and frowned. Slaves. A powerful sense of déjà vu consumed him.

Niccoli walked toward the mansion, apparently not catching Stone's discomfort, and dismissed Andor with a wave of his hand. The Viking and the group of isen peeled away, heading for one of the smaller, manor homes.

"Where are they going?" Stone asked.

"To Andor's manor. I award homes to my children who in turn create many isen children of their own. Perhaps, you may have one too, Stone, if you can keep up with the Viking."

Stone didn't answer. He had no intention of staying here that long, much less turning another isen unless it could fuel his experiments.

Niccoli climbed the porch to the mansion, and the door opened from within. A woman stood on the other side, pressed to the wall, eyes on the floor with one arm extended to invite them inside. Niccoli passed without a word, and Stone followed.

Vivienne leaned in and whispered. "She must be one of the slaves."

Stone flinched. He'd forgotten his child isen was there.

The hallway went on for quite a while, and several open doors lined the walls. Stone peeked in each as he passed—dining area, office, sitting room, library.

He paused. Library?

He twisted around and peeked in. Sure enough, books lined floor-to-ceiling shelves across all four walls. The door, a window, and a fireplace served as the only gaps in the mountain of books. Several chairs filled the space, some facing the fireplace and some the window, but all were empty.

Stone smiled. At least he would be at home here until he could find a way to run away. He resolved to escape to a place with as many or more books. It would be crucial to his studies.

"I assumed you would like this," Niccoli said, once more at Stone's side.

"It's magnificent."

"Put your books away. You may borrow whatever you like, but always return it."

Stone frowned. "But you gave me those books."

"Everything is mine. You simply borrow."

Annoyance rippled through him. All his beautiful books, stowed away for morons to touch. All this time, he'd thought he'd been building a collection of his own when in fact, he'd been building Niccoli's library.

"I will do it later," Stone lied.

"Now," Niccoli ordered.

Stone grumbled under his breath and looked for a gap in the books. To the left of the fireplace, he was able to push several of the novels aside and slip the few he'd gathered in Paris between them. The only two he kept for himself were his journal and the book he'd stolen from the manor lord all those years ago.

He stood, disgusted with himself.

"There's one more," Niccoli said.

Stone spun around, confused. "That's all of them."

"You didn't put *the Anglo-Saxon Chronicles* away with the rest."

"But that one's mine! I've had it since before you turned me!"

Niccoli smirked and repeated what he'd said once already. "Everything is mine. You simply borrow."

Stone bristled, but his master's smirk became a glare. He wouldn't win a battle with Niccoli. He *never* won against Niccoli.

He knelt and pulled his beloved book from his bag, grateful that his journal, at least, was a secret. With the food, quills, and ink he'd stowed in the bag, perhaps Niccoli wouldn't notice the journal's weight when Stone stood. He slipped his book in with the rest and rose, back to the wall so as not to give Niccoli a chance to see the contents of his bag.

"When may I leave to explore Ourea?" Stone asked.

Niccoli shook his head. "You must stay here."

"But—"

Niccoli turned to the hall. "Anita!"

The woman who had opened the door returned, eyes still on the floor. Niccoli said something to her in what Stone assumed was Russian, which he hadn't yet learned. In that moment, Stone resolved to learn it in secret. He would know every language his master knew, and the man would never again keep secrets if Stone could help it.

Niccoli walked out without another word, and the girl curtsied to Stone and Vivienne before gesturing toward the hall and walking out. Stone assumed that meant to follow and obliged her with Vivienne in tow.

They meandered through the halls, Stone too angry to pay much attention, and climbed a set of stairs. She stopped at a door and pushed it open before taking Vivienne's hand and leading her farther down the hall.

Stone stepped into what he assumed was his room and shut the door behind him. A bed sat against the far wall, a window above it to let in what light filtered through the canopy outside. Other than that, the room's only decoration was a wide dresser that filled most of the wall to his right.

He leaned on the door and rubbed his face. He needed to remain rational. Calm. But all he wanted to do was hurt someone, preferably Niccoli. Coming to Ourea wouldn't help him if he was stuck within the confines of the guild. It was exactly like Paris—trapped with no access to real magic.

This wasn't a life worth living, and Stone couldn't take much more of it.

10

EXPERIMENT

July, 904 A.D.
Niccoli's Guild

Stone crept down the stairs. Each step resulted in a creak he could barely hear, but he wasn't going to take any chances. He kept to the edges of the stairway, careful not to make noise as he stole through Niccoli's house. It would never be home, and he didn't intend to stay long enough to feel comfortable. But while he was here, he needed to take care of what troubled him most.

On the first floor, no one passed him. He stole through the paneled hallway, straining his ears for the slightest warning he had company. Nothing came.

The library doors were closed when he reached them. He twisted the handle ever so slowly, careful not to let it squeak. He inched the door open and examined the room. Moonlight cast a pale glow over the chairs and bookshelves. An ember burned in the fireplace, piles of ashes surrounding it, and the familiar tome that cost him his human life sat on a shelf beside it. He crept toward it and knelt.

Perhaps it wouldn't do him any good, but he needed to hide *the Anglo-Saxon Chronicles* for his own sake. He searched the bookshelves until he found a corner of the room with several books that had similar covers, all of which were covered in dust. He could only hope no one would look for it here, even though he suspected Niccoli would search for this tome in particular. He studied it in its new home, sitting on a vile man's shelf, and that twinge of disgust burned brighter in his chest.

This book belonged to Stone. He'd died for it.

He left the room before he had the chance to do something he would inevitably regret and closed the door behind him, careful not to make a sound as he walked down the hall. He once more took the stairs and crept along the edges to avoid squeaky steps.

But when he opened his bedroom door, someone waited for him on his bed.

Vivienne looked up as he entered, tears in her eyes. A few had dripped down her face, leaving a trail in their wake.

He grimaced. "What is it?"

"I just wanted company," she said.

"I'm told I'm not very good company."

She nodded. "But you're all I have right now, so you will have to do."

Stone hesitated, curious as to whether or not that should offend him. After a moment, he shrugged away the thought. "Very well."

He sat on the bed and set his elbows on his knees, intertwining his fingers together as he wondered what exactly she wanted. They sat in silence. Moonlight broke through the window in beams, illuminating dust on the floor. A few streaks on the floorboards revealed where he'd walked and where her skirt had dragged along the floor as she'd entered.

"What are we?" she asked, her voice quiet.

"Isen. I already told you."

She shook her head. "I mean what are we? Why do isen exist? How do we exist? We're unnatural."

"Hardly. Neither of us had any say in this matter. We are what we are."

"Then why haven't I heard of isen before today?"

"The world is full of things we haven't heard of before today. That's what makes it so interesting."

Her brows furrowed, and she shook her head. "I'm just trying to understand, and you're not helping."

"I suggest you get used to that."

She laughed through a sob, and Stone wasn't sure why.

They once more sat in silence, Stone staring at the

floor as he lost himself in thought. His mind raced back to his precious book. It held the stories of kings and invaders, revolutions and wars lost. It didn't belong in a commoner's library. He'd learned about war theory from this book, and—

He sat up straighter. Vivienne flinched, but he barely noticed.

His book had given him so many ideas, and it occurred to him that there was one lesson in particular he could use. In war, the stronger side usually won unless the weaker side did something clever. And that was what he had to do: something clever to escape until he could somehow become stronger than Niccoli.

A flurry of excitement bubbled within him. He needed to test how far the beacon could stretch. When he knew its weaknesses, he could exploit them and perhaps even escape Niccoli once and for all.

But he'd been banned from leaving, which complicated his plan. His lip quivered, and he rubbed his cheek in frustration. Unless ...

He eyed Vivienne. Yes, *he* had been banned. Not her. Perhaps he could still run his experiments after all.

Using her meant he would have to be patient, which didn't suit him. He would, however, be as patient as possible and wait as long as it took if it meant freedom.

"I have an experiment to run on you," Stone said.

"Good Lord, no more questions for Death!"

He waved the thought away with his hand. "This is much better."

She huffed and crossed her arms, leaning back on the bed and refusing to look at him. "Out with it."

"I want you to leave the guild."

She let out a huff of air. "But we just got here!"

"Niccoli won't let me leave, as we saw today. But he seems to care much less about you, and we can use that to our advantage. I will play the good boy and do whatever Niccoli wants in an effort to distract him long enough to let you slip in and out of the guild."

"What will that tell us?"

"I can sense you anywhere. If I listen for it, I know exactly where you are, what floor of a house you're on, and if you're moving. I call it the beacon."

She shuddered.

Stone continued. "What I want to test, then, is whether or not I can feel you when you pass into Earth from Ourea. I want to know how strong this beacon is, how far it goes, and, perhaps, even how I can break it. You will need to go far and wide, in and out of Earth, and return consistently. That way, no one will get suspicious, and no one will go out looking for you. They need to think you're doing my research for me, going out and collecting specimens and the like."

She rubbed her arms. "But I've never traveled. I've never even left Paris. And there are even parts of Paris I have never been to."

"Then learn."

She grimaced and let out a breath, her nose wrinkling as if she smelled something foul. "How on Earth am I supposed to learn something like that by myself?"

Stone let out an exasperated sigh. "Stop playing the victim. You are more than capable, judging by what I saw before I turned you, not to mention what happened afterward. You bit Andor, for Christ's sake. You escaped the ropes I used to tie you down. You screamed bloody murder when I woke you up to ask you the questions for Death. You are by no means a weak woman, Vivienne, and you will find a way."

She watched him, her eyes pinched and a bit wet at the corners. Her lips parted ever so slightly, and she didn't reply.

Stone continued. "This is your chance to make your own life, albeit one helping me. Don't for one second try to be the victim. I already know you better than that."

"You believe in me?" she asked, her voice the barest whisper.

"Obviously. Don't ask stupid questions."

She laughed and wiped away a tear. "You're such an inspiration."

Stone paused, curious as to whether or not that was sarcastic, but ultimately plowed onward. "Start small with a trip back to Paris, though be sure no one recognizes you. I recommend you steal a soul while you're there, one who seems useful in some way, preferably a good fighter or thief. Someone whose skills you can use."

"And how do I do that?"

"I'll draw you a diagram and include instructions on how to steal a soul. I warn you, though, the first time is unpleasant."

"I—what?"

"Of course," Stone continued, ignoring her, "It would be better if I was there with you, but that does not seem to be an option. I trust you to find someone useful. Use those skills to explore Paris. Find maps, steal any potions or concoctions you can find, and come back when you're done."

"But—"

"Go to bed. Get some sleep for now, and you'll leave tomorrow. In the meantime, I'll draft up as much of a map as I can remember to lead you back. Go on, off with you."

She stood but didn't step toward the door.

"What is it?" he asked, annoyed.

"I'm nervous, and I don't know if I can do this, but thank you for trusting me."

What an odd remark. He didn't have many options when it came to who he could trust, and since he could control her, she didn't pose much of a threat. Obviously, her comment came from something else, possibly her relationship with her father, but he didn't very much care.

With a nod to dismiss her, he kept his eyes on the floor, eager for her to leave so he could get his journal out again. No one could know about his journal, not even her, and he doubted she remembered it from her brief moment of consciousness when he'd asked her to memorize questions for Death.

His door opened and closed, and the beacon in his chest told him she'd begun down the hallway. He let out a quiet sigh and reached for the journal under his pillow, grateful he no longer had to share a room. As he drew the map, a quiet flicker of hope burned in his chest. He had to be careful not to get his hopes up, though, because there was a very real chance this would not work at all.

The next day, Stone sat on the porch, waving goodbye with a forced smile as Vivienne walked toward the exit armed with nothing but a pack of food slung over her shoulder and Stone's scribbled notes tucked into her waistline.

The farewell was for show, and it seemed like an obvious trick to him. He merely hoped it seemed natural to others. He feared the sendoff was inauthentic—perhaps his smile was too wide, as he didn't do it often—but he doubted anyone really cared. The only isen watching him and Vivienne were the guards posted by the exit, and they had their eyes on him instead of her. That was the goal. Attract attention and let her slip by without notice.

A hand smacked his shoulder and shook him a bit in welcome. Niccoli appeared at his side, likely from the house. Yet again, Stone hadn't heard him at all, nor felt him approach, and it irked him that he had no way of keeping tabs on his master.

"Where is your child going?" Niccoli asked.

Stone crossed his arms. "She's running some experiments for me, since you won't let me leave."

"Keep an eye on her. I would hate to have to punish her for deserting." With that, Niccoli left. This time, floorboards creaked under his feet as his footsteps retreated into the house.

Stone stiffened. He'd never heard of a deserter, nor Niccoli's apparent policy on punishing escapees when they were found. Regardless, Stone was confident Vivienne would return. He crossed his arms, and as she walked out of sight, the beacon moved with her. Even as she retreated farther and farther away, the beacon didn't dim in the slightest.

He did, however, feel something else.

As her skirt swished around the bend and out of view, a discomfort settled into his chest. An ache, almost, like something had suddenly gone missing from within his body.

He scratched his chest, trying to rid himself of the sensation, but it remained. Puzzled, he tried to dissect it. Perhaps, his breakfast had contained old meat, or worse, perhaps he'd contracted a cold, or—

His mouth dropped open, and he stood straighter with the sudden realization that it wasn't food or illness. It hadn't begun until that blasted Frenchwoman faded from sight, and it grew stronger the farther she walked. For the first time in his life, Stone missed the company of another person. And he didn't like it at all.

11

THE BOND

Stone stood in Niccoli's study, hands on the man's desk as he loomed over a map. Niccoli stood by a row of windows, staring out over his domain with his hands behind his back. Stone occasionally snuck glances at his master to gauge his mood. His disdain for the isen had only grown over the last six decades.

Sixty-three years. Stone had endured. He had obeyed. And he was running out of patience. He scanned the room, anxious for anything he could use in his pursuit of an escape, but the empty shelves taunted him, daring him to ask Niccoli for the books he knew must be hidden. Though the library held interesting information, none of it furthered Stone's cause. The office must have held useful books, maps, and knowledge that could give him his key to finally gaining his freedom, but he'd never found it. He rarely had the chance to look.

"I would like to search Spain next," Niccoli said.

New isen. For all these years, Stone had been forced to march alongside Niccoli as he went in and out of the human world, collecting isen for his ever-growing army. They now had thousands of isen in the guild. He didn't know when the man would have enough, and he had long ago resigned himself to the never-ending task.

But Niccoli was not alone in his pursuit.

Stone shook his head. "There are already seven, competing isen guilds in Spain, and a dwindling supply of unawaken isen. It would be best to head east toward Palermo, the capital of the Emirate of Sicily. Less attention has been placed on the east, and we would have the advantage."

In the years since arriving to Ourea, Stone had often debated becoming useless. He figured if he didn't give good answers, Niccoli would stop asking questions. Stone could make himself obsolete, and when he was no longer needed, he would be allowed to roam Ourea as Niccoli had promised all those years ago. That was the theory, anyway, and Stone was too smart to think it would work. He'd proven himself too useful over the years, and at this point, Niccoli could always force him to speak. If Stone ever became too much of a burden, Niccoli would probably kill him before letting him go.

"When will you have enough?" Stone asked. His hand tightened around the edge of the desk to brace himself as he asked the question that had burned in him for years.

"What do you mean?"

"Isen. It's been almost seventy years since I started helping you. When will you have enough of them? When will you be done?"

Niccoli turned far enough for Stone to see his face. The man's dark eyebrows pinched together, and the edge of his mouth turned up in a slight sneer. "One day, I will be the largest and most powerful isen in Ourea. To have power, one must amass it. There will never be enough."

"But we've already cleared another area for houses. We're running out of room."

"Then we clear more. The slaves do the work. I'm not sure why this concerns you."

Niccoli met his eye, but Stone did not back down. His patience waned with each day, and he could not take much more of this.

But instead of a confrontation, his master returned his stare to the window. Stone let out a breath.

"I'll be more useful if I have time to rest. May I leave

to explore Ourea? I'll need a month at most, or even a few weeks—"

"Every time you ask, I say no. Yet you continue asking," Niccoli said.

"Eventually, you will say yes. You said yourself you won't need me forever."

"Then wait for that day to come. Stop asking."

The order churned in Stone's gut, more than words. It was a command, one he could not disobey. He frowned and stared at the floor. "Do you need anything else?"

"No. We'll leave in a few days. Try not to waste your time until we do."

An hour later, Stone sat in his room, back against the wall as he stared out at the yard below. He scratched his chest, trying to satiate the emptiness that gnawed at him when Vivienne was away. Below, a group of men, dressed in the beige slacks of the slaves, dragged wheat along the ground on their way to the mill in another part of the labyrinth of interconnecting clearings that composed Niccoli's Guild. Even from several stories in the air, Stone could see the grimaces on their faces. He'd never had to haul wheat for the manor lord, but he remembered the lads who did. They had all worn those expressions, too. He cleared his throat, an uncomfortable pressure in his chest at the thought. Although he didn't look a day older than when he himself was a slave, he tried very hard to push those memories to the farthest reaches of his mind. It didn't work.

On his way into the room, he'd lifted his sword from where it hung by his door and carried it with him to his bed. He now lifted the weapon in his hands, examining its sharp edges and deadly tip. He never used it, his decoration, so it still seemed fairly new. Still sharp. Still deadly.

Perhaps it could make itself useful.

He wondered if he could do it—kill himself. He thought about it more and more often, lately. Though Niccoli had seemed distracted earlier, Stone still knew better than to think he could simply walk out. No amount of distraction seemed enough to keep Niccoli's mind from wandering far enough away to allow for the moment of weakness that would let Stone escape.

With no other choices, death seemed like the best option... at least, that was, until he heard from Vivienne. And he always did, time and time again, even when months went by without her return. She would always, without fail, come back. And when she did, his thoughts would shift from suicide to freedom. The itch in his chest would dissolve, and he would finally be able to return to his work.

He enjoyed the Frenchwoman and her insights on

Ourean theory. When she started, she could barely draw a map, but her skill improved each time. She always had a fresh idea, sometimes even one he hadn't thought of first himself. She was far more enjoyable than Andor, and certainly more entertaining than anyone else in the guild. But each time he sent her on a new expedition, the damned itch would return in his chest, and he would be reminded of his dependence on another person. He loathed it. The itch made him a slave to her, in a way, because it served as an emotional tether to another living creature. He actually cared if she lived or died; where that had come from, he couldn't fathom. He didn't want to take her to bed like Andor seduced his women, or even touch her for that matter. The thought alone made Stone gag—such nonsense was nothing more than distraction. He and Vivienne simply discussed theory. Plotted their escape. Dissected the laws of magic.

Although Stone was her master, Vivienne somehow owned a part of him. And he hated it.

He thought he'd felt her enter Ourea a few days ago, but she'd blipped in and out so quickly he doubted himself. She must have passed through Ourea to go elsewhere.

At least her beacon could disappear. When they'd first begun their experiments, Stone worried that he could sense her always—more importantly, that Niccoli could sense him always. But the beacon faded.

Over long distances, it grew fainter and fainter until it faded completely. And anytime she passed into the human realm from Ourea, he lost her altogether. It was good news; news that gave them hope for his eventual escape. If he could get far enough away, Niccoli might never find him.

Might. Maybe. There were too many variables for Stone's taste.

But never, not once, could she feel him, and that worried Stone the most. He needed to be able to sense Niccoli, to run if need be, because as long as he could sense Vivienne's beacon, however faintly, he could control her. Even from a distance.

He dragged the tip of his finger along the swords point, drawing blood in a thin line that dripped over the blade. Pain rippled up his hand and into his elbow, but he ignored it. If he could do that, perhaps it wouldn't be too hard to go farther.

He'd run out of patience. He'd run out of information. He'd run out of options, too—he could either wait for Vivienne, or be done with it all.

But what would become of her? He stiffened and lowered his sword. Most likely, Niccoli would kill her out of spite. Stone rubbed the stubble on his chin, his blood smearing in the hair. He marveled that he could care so much about whether or not that happened. Of all the people in his life, Vivienne annoyed him the least. He would prefer she live. Even after all these years, his heart ached each time she left.

He would never confess any of that nonsense to her, of course. It might distract her research, and it meant nothing. To be lonely …

Stone picked up the sword once more and examined the blade, retracing in his mind all of his attempts to discover more about Ourea. He'd read every book in the library at least once, many of them twice, but none carried much information beyond what he'd already gleaned. He'd learned Russian in secret, but Niccoli sometimes spoke too fast for Stone to understand, and it frustrated him to no end. Vivienne would sneak in books for him from her travels, and even taught him some of the native languages of Ourea, including the common tongue of Ethosian. She'd drawn him maps of her adventures, laying out an ever-growing visualization of Ourea and its connection to the human realm.

But none of it pieced together. None of it helped him.

He lifted the blade to his throat, careful to place the sharpest edge against his neck. He sat there, the metal denting his skin, and debated his options. Its cold weight leaned into him, quiet and waiting for the order only he could give. He stared at the hilt, debating …

A tingle crept along his spine, alerting him that Vivienne had once more entered Ourea. Her beacon burned like a bonfire, loud and close. She would arrive in about twenty minutes, thirty minutes if she had extra books weighing down her pack.

He stood and slid the sword back into its sheath, which still hung by the door. Perhaps another time, then.

§✤

Stone sat on his bed, legs crossed as he waited for Vivienne to enter his room any minute now. It was the only safe place for them to speak, as it was the only place no one bothered them. Niccoli must have assumed the relationship was more than it was and wanted to give them space to produce more isen for him. Stone would let the man think what he pleased if it meant he had privacy. At least Stone's chest no longer itched, now that he could sense her beacon, and he had to admit his gratitude at her return.

Two knocks vibrated against the door, but the person on the other side didn't wait for him to speak. She let herself in and shut the door behind her with a swish of her skirt.

Vivienne smiled in welcome, as she did every time, though Stone offered nothing in return. Brown smudges on her face hid her smooth skin, but Stone figured many men would find her attractive even while filthy. She hadn't aged a day since he'd found her. Several dark purple stains littered the bodice of her traveling gown, and a tear in her skirt revealed the pants she wore underneath.

"What did you do to yourself?" Stone asked.

"I was in a bit of a brawl on the way home. Some muggers attacked me, but their souls weren't worth stealing. I just killed them."

Stone smirked. It was hard to remember a time where he could have drugged and smothered her. She'd certainly become useful.

"I have a gift for you," she said. She tossed the pack onto the bed and nodded to it.

He unlaced the bag and lifted it by its bottom, spilling its contents onto the bed. Five books fell out, all of them wrapped in blue binding.

"Lossian books," Vivienne said with a grin.

He frowned a little. Lossians were yakona, and even though people of the five yakona kingdoms all looked different, Lossians intrigued him the most. They walked on two legs like a human, but their blue skin, giant heads, and massive eyes always left him stunned for a moment. He'd seen a few drawings of them, but never met one in person.

"Topics?" he asked.

She smirked. "They're all written about the blood loyalty."

Stone smiled, grateful, and couldn't believe his luck. Yakona had a blood loyalty to their monarchs, one so painfully similar to Niccoli's connection that it left

Stone wondering how similar Ourea's various creatures truly were. For Stone, he had to obey his master, Niccoli. For the yakona, they had to obey their Blood, or king. Perhaps in studying their connection, Stone could unravel his own.

Stone picked up the nearest book and examined it. The author's name stared back at him in silver lettering:

Benir Udrenit.

Good, it was a language he could read. He enjoyed Ethosian.

"You've outdone yourself," Stone said.

She laughed. "That's the closest thing to a thank you I've ever heard out of your mouth."

He didn't answer. Instead, he picked up another book and noticed its author. Udrenit yet again. His name was on all the books, in fact. "Who is this man?"

"The same one who made this." She pulled a folded piece of parchment out of a pocket in her skirt. With a grin, she handed it to Stone.

Stone took it and unfolded the paper to reveal a massive map. Its precise lines, the multiple colors of ink... a flutter of joy burned in his chest as he realized this was the first map she'd given him that she had not drawn herself. He knelt and spread it along the floor to examine it. Though Niccoli kept all maps hidden, Stone had amassed several, thanks to Vivienne's travels. He had by no means collected the entire map of

Ourea, and he often pondered how massive this land must be.

Although this couldn't be all of Ourea, as it omitted the Rose Cliffs and several other landmarks he knew to exist, it depicted a section Stone barely recognized. A black X in the middle of a large forest sat beside a glowing, blue triangle. Outlines of mountains and forests covered much of the map, with lakes, streams, and a smattering of ponds filling the rest. More blue triangles filled the map, all of them glittering with a life of their own despite the limited sunlight available in his room.

Vivienne pointed to the X. "I did this. This is the guild, where we are now."

"And this triangle?" Stone asked.

"Lichgate. Isn't it marvelous how they glow? No one would show me how he did it."

Stone rubbed his chin, marveling at the sheer number of portals. At least twenty triangles filled the map. "All of these are lichgates?"

"All of them."

"Amazing. There are so many."

"And this is only a small part of Ourea. A map of the lands near this township of Adenot." She pointed to a circle at the center of the map. It sat close to Niccoli's guild—about a day's walk if he had to guess. Closer than any yakona creature should be to a hive of isen, at any rate.

Vivienne must have noticed what he was staring at. "I found out that you can make it there in just a few hours if you take this lichgate", she pointed at one of the triangles, "and one more after that. I can show you."

"Do they know of us?" he asked.

"It doesn't seem so. I don't think they'd stay if they did. My guess is Niccoli likes being close in case he needs supplies or an emergency magical soul."

"Logical."

"Can I share a theory with you?" she asked.

Stone nodded.

"My guess is Ourea's a single world. These lichgates make it easy to jump between places, and thus no one I've run into has a full map without jumps. It's easier to connect the lichgates, I suppose. It's just a hunch, though."

"A good one, I suspect," Stone said, his focus still on the map.

"I do believe that was a compliment," Vivienne said.

He could almost hear the smile in her voice. He ignored it. "Where did you get this?"

"In another Lossian town farther south from here. It's off the map. But here's the best part. Udrenit—the author of all those books, lives here." She tapped the circle marking the township of Adenot.

Stone nodded. "Have you met this author?"

"Not personally."

"Is he well known for his work?"

She nodded. "The word is he was once invited to the palace by the Lossian Blood himself to discuss his research."

Stone rubbed his chin, intrigued. "I'll go through his books. If he seems useful, perhaps we should pay him a visit."

Her eyebrows shot up. "We?"

"It's been ten years since I last stole a soul, and I think it's high time I found a useful one instead of the slaves Niccoli feeds me here."

She wrung her hands, eyebrows twisting. "He's a prominent figure, Stone. People will notice if he goes missing. You won't be able to blend into a crowd, or—"

"How often do I need to blend into Lossian crowds? Humans, maybe, but it doesn't matter here. If the books are useful, we're going. It's not a discussion."

She pursed her lips but nodded. "Fine. Brute."

Stone picked up the nearest Lossian tome and flipped open to the first page. He laid his back on the floor and propped his legs on the bed.

Vivienne sighed, but Stone barely registered the sound.

"We'll talk later then, I suppose," she said.

He didn't answer. He'd assumed that was obvious.

Hollow steps tapped along the wooden floor, and the door clicked shut. Stone settled into his book, but Vivienne's beacon moved through the house. He smiled, happy the itch was finally gone.

12

THE SCHOLAR

August, 967 A.D.
Niccoli's Guild

S tone crossed his arms and arched his back, refusing to budge from his spot by the door in Niccoli's office. Across the room, a beam of sunlight shone on Niccoli's scowl. The isen master glared, eyebrows furrowed in their standoff.

"You may not leave the guild," Niccoli said again, teeth clenched so tightly that his accent became almost unintelligible.

Stone tilted his head in mock annoyance, trying to play the part that would get him enough leave to visit the author Vivienne had found him. "I'm not asking to leave for long. I'm going to get a soul. My decade is up, and I need another to keep from aging, same as every isen here."

"So, choose a slave. I have hundreds. You've done it before."

Stone grimaced. Yes, he had, but only out of necessity. He'd never known other villages were so close. "I want someone worth stealing. Someone useful."

"Who do you have in mind?"

Stone paused. This was the tricky part, the bit he wasn't sure would work. He'd read through all of the scholar's books twice, everything Vivienne had given him, and he suspected Udrenit's soul would give him the information he needed to break his loyalty to Niccoli. The problem was, he didn't know if Niccoli knew of Udrenit's work. He had to make this trip seem worth the effort, without revealing his true plan.

Thus, his dilemma.

"In reading the books in your library, I've discovered a local Lossian town," Stone lied. "Rumor has it, there are scholars there, souls with interesting information about Ourea and its magic. Since you won't let me leave, they're the next best thing."

Niccoli lifted his chin, eyes widening as if he'd understood something hidden in the lie. This new expression tested Stone. His skin itched, and his eyes stung with the desire to look away. Instead, he cleared his throat and kept his gaze up, knowing full well that

if he betrayed even the barest hint of a lie, he'd probably be chained to his room for eternity. Or worse.

His master's eyes narrowed, and frown lines
appeared in the man's brow. "Anything else?"

Stone forced himself to frown and continue his lie.
"What do you mean? Is there something about this
town I should know?"

Niccoli clamped his jaw shut with an audible click,
as if he'd said too much. Stone resisted the impulse
to smirk.

"Be back by sundown," Niccoli said. He turned his
back and stared out the window.

Stone nodded even though the isen could no longer
see him and retreated, barely able to hide the smile on
his face. He was leaving the guild—alone. He could
barely believe it.

Vivienne had promised to wait for him on the
porch, so he pushed open the front door of the
mansion to find her. Its hinges creaked. Vivienne
jumped, hand resting on her chest as she leaned onto
the porch railing in a blue traveling gown. The shade
fought for attention against her black curls and pale
skin; in all honesty, it didn't suit her at all. The bodice
dipped too low along her chest, in Stone's opinion, but
he refrained from commenting on it.

"What did he say?" she asked, her face pale. She
wrung her hands and shifted her weight three times in
the few seconds it took for her to speak.

Stone leaned in and spoke under his breath. "Try to contain yourself. You look like a startled rabbit."

She cleared her throat and smoothed her skirts, eyes darting to the side. The worry lines dissolved from her brow. "Better?"

"Much. We're leaving."

A smile broke across her face, and her eyes lit with excitement. Stone frowned, and she once more cleared her throat to hide her joy.

Stone walked down the steps and headed for the tunnel that would take them out of the guild, Vivienne right behind him. He kept his eyes ahead even as he monitored his surroundings from his peripheral vision. Several isen sitting on the nearest manor porch looked up from their conversations, heads turned in his direction.

"Hello, Stone," a gruff voice said from behind him.

Stone stopped in his tracks and let out a heavy sigh. He knew that voice. "You don't need to join us, Andor."

Andor pulled ahead and set his massive hands on his hips. "We both know that's not true. Niccoli wouldn't let you wander off, even to steal a soul."

"And you're his watchdog? I thought you had a mind of your own."

Vivienne gasped, but Stone didn't pay her any mind.

Andor frowned and leaned in, his frame looming over Stone's like a storm cloud that blocked out the light. "Not even you may speak to me like that."

The stink of garlic and something foul—rancid meat, maybe—blended with the Viking's breath. Stone held his breath, too close to the man's mouth for comfort, but he refused to budge even as his cheeks flushed with the desire to vomit.

Andor continued toward the tunnel. "Let's not waste daylight."

"You aren't needed," Stone insisted.

"I'm following orders. Someone needs to watch over you, and I'm the only one who can stand you. But you're testing even me at the moment."

Stone clenched his fists. He should have known this would happen, should have planned for it. Maybe he was getting sloppy.

This new development disrupted his plan.

Finally, after several moments of frustrated tension, he stomped along behind the Viking. Once more Vivienne followed, barely making enough sound to be his shadow.

Light dissolved as they entered the tunnel that would take them out of the guild. Lanterns strung overhead illuminated the way, and isen guards sat in the branches every few yards as lookouts. They watched Stone—he could feel their eyes on the back of his neck—but he wouldn't do them the service of glancing up.

"So, what are you really up to?" Andor whispered.

"I'm retrieving a soul. My ten years are up."

Andor huffed and lumbered on ahead, boots crunching the dirt as he led the way.

Stone's mind raced. He would need time to sift through the scholar's thoughts, perhaps even visit the Lossian's home to look for books or other information that would help him. After killing a prominent figure, he would never be able to return to the village, and that meant he had one chance to find any necessary books or artifacts to help him. One. And to make matters worse, it would take time to discover where those things were—time Andor likely wouldn't give him without an excuse. The Viking would betray everything he did to Niccoli, and thus, Stone had to tread with care.

So, he lied again.

"We're also stopping for a Lossian beer to welcome Vivienne home." He watched her out of the corner of his eye, gauging her reaction. Her dark eyes widened in the second after he spoke, but she erupted in a smile only he could tell was fake. Her eyes pinched together too much, and the lines around her lips creased too deeply to be authentic.

"It's about time, too!" she added.

Andor laughed. "I don't believe that at all."

Stone shrugged and continued the lie. "It's true."

"Why would you want a Lossian beer?" Andor asked.

Vivienne shrugged. "They're not that bad."

The Viking pointed to Stone. "But he doesn't drink beer. Or celebrate. Or do nice things for people."

"There's a first for everything," Vivienne said.

Andor chuckled.

Stone sighed. These two would likely chat the whole trip. He couldn't be afforded one second of silence. It wasn't fair.

It took an hour of hiking and two lichgates, but Stone finally made it to the ocean with Andor and Vivienne in tow. The Viking wouldn't shut up, but at least Vivienne fielded most of the conversation, which left Stone to his, admittedly, interrupted thoughts.

Despite their jabbering, he'd formulated a new plan, one to accommodate Andor's unwelcome presence— they would find this scholar, steal his soul, and go to a pub. There, Stone would be able to sift through the Lossian's thoughts while Vivienne continued to occupy the Viking long enough for Stone to discover where the scholar kept his most valuable information. They would steal what they could—in the name of Niccoli, of course—and Stone would sneak away to find the most precious books on the Blood loyalty. Hopefully, he would be able to convey this to Vivienne without Andor discovering what he was up to. He needed her to distract the Viking as much as possible.

Waves crashed far below against the cliffside. The forest behind him, which held the lichgate they'd used to cross into this land, had a thick canopy that hid the underbrush in shadow. The cliff snaked away on either side of him, sudden and steep. The bite of salty air left an aftertaste on his tongue. He grimaced.

He'd brought Vivienne's map, but he didn't dare look at it in Andor's presence. He wasn't supposed to keep things from Niccoli—anything at all—and he certainly wanted to keep Vivienne's gifts a secret. He had to rely on memory, which would be fine. He'd stared at it enough since she had given it to him that he could likely go by memory.

"We need to go this way," Andor said, pointing back to the forest.

Stone frowned. Perhaps he wouldn't need to. "How do you know where we're going?"

Andor shook his head. "It's the only Lossian town nearby. Don't play stupid."

Vivienne caught Stone's eye and shrugged.

"Fine," Stone said.

The trio marched toward the woods, and the crashing waves faded as they passed under the thick leaves of the forest. Eventually, only the chirps of birds in the canopy kept them company. At least his companions had finally stopped chatting.

Hundreds of dark blue flowers appeared in the underbrush, bunched together. Dozens of flowers clumped together on single stalks, their six, long petals curved backward in an arch.

"Hyacinth flowers," Vivienne whispered, apparently watching his eyes.

"That's nice," Stone said.

"They mask the isen scent," she added.

This piqued Stone's interest. "Do they, now?"

"Niccoli had them planted around all," Andor cleared his throat and cast a sideways glance to Stone, "um, this nearby village to mask our natural scent in the event we visit."

Stone resisted the impulse to grimace. Of course, there were more towns nearby.

Vivienne grinned. "It's genius really! Planting a scent-hiding flower that the locals think is native growth, when really ..."

Stone caught her eye and frowned, disappointed in his protégée for her apparent admiration of the man he loathed. She trailed off, and her smile faded as she resumed her silent march.

Andor crouched, half of his body now submerged in the sea of hyacinth flowers near a thick trunk. Vivienne followed, though only her head appeared of her above the petals. Stone followed suit, crouching without touching his knees to the soil. He balanced his weight on his fingertips.

Ahead lay a swamp full of clear water unlike any Stone had read about in his books. Although it could have been a lake, trees jutted from it as if it were soil. White pods lay in the water, three times the height of a man, and each had holes for doors and windows. They seemed to have been baked from the earth like a single, hollow brick made from chalk. They rounded at the top, and there were no decorations of any kind. Nothing but white stone and holes.

A Lossian trudged through the water not far off. His blue form slogged through the waist-high water. His black pants stuck to his thin legs, and he wore no shirt. His bald, blue head turned away from them so that, unfortunately, Stone couldn't see the creature's face.

Stone grinned. Fascinating. Blue skin, bald heads. If the drawings were accurate, they even had massive eyes one third the size of their faces. He inched forward, eager to find his scholar.

"Who do you have in mind?" Andor asked. The same question Niccoli had asked.

"A scholar," Stone answered.

"Which—"

Vivienne interrupted. "I'll get one for you."

Stone bristled. "I don't need to be fed, thank you."

Andor grabbed Stone's collar and tugged, sending him onto his rump. The wet soil seeped into his pants, and Stone muttered under his breath as he brushed away the dirt.

"Stay out of trouble," Andor said.

Vivienne closed her eyes, and her form shifted. Cracks appeared in her pale skin, and blue scales shone below them. Thousands of tiny scales littered her body as her old skin fell away in flakes that dissolved into powder as they touched the flowers. Her head grew, and her spine stretched. Even her eyes expanded until they were wide, green orbs that glistened. Black hair spiraled from her head in curls and stopped below her neck. Her dress stretched with her, a little tighter once she'd completed the transformation.

"I'll be back in a little while," she said. Her voice warbled as if she were speaking underwater.

Stone couldn't help himself. He grinned. These creatures fascinated him, even if this one was only a mask.

Vivienne stood and walked into the water, hands hovering above the surface as she plowed ahead. Her skirts floated behind her, billowing in the currents she created. In minutes, she disappeared around the farthest pod he could see and faded from sight.

And, as had happened every time she walked away, the void appeared once more in Stone's chest. He swallowed hard and tried to push it away—she would be back soon, after all—but it lingered all the same.

"Now we wait," Andor said. He kept his eyes on the forest, switching between water and woods as he kept an eye out.

Stone, on the other hand, gave up and sat on the

ground. The moisture from over-watered soil seeped into his pants yet again, but he'd already ruined them. He might as well not tire his legs by crouching.

Ten minutes passed. Twenty. The moisture seeping into Stone's britches spread through the fabric, creating a circle of discomfort that left dew on his skin. He grimaced, but it wouldn't do any good to stand at this point.

Andor cracked his knuckles. "She should be back by now."

"She's fine," Stone said without looking up.

"Something happened. I should go find her."

"Nonsense." Stone supposed she was searching for the author to the books she'd brought him, and he expected that to take time. Andor, however, couldn't be allowed to know she'd gone after a specific man.

Andor huffed. "If that was one of my children, I would have left to find her five minutes ago. You hardly seem worried at all. Luring away a soul shouldn't take this long, Stone, not with her level of experience. Something went wrong; I know it. Maybe they discovered what she is. She could be dead. Do you even care?"

A pang in Stone's chest lit an unknown emotion within his core. It bubbled, almost like a pot of boiling water, festering in his stomach. His shoulders and back tensed, so much so that he frowned on impulse. "Don't say stupid things, Andor!"

The Viking paused for a moment, face blank. It seemed almost as if he were confused, but he broke out into laughter. His eyes crinkled with delight. "If I didn't know better, I'd say you're offended."

Stone chewed on the word. Not much offended him —he'd have to care for something to offend him, and he cared about so little. But Vivienne—yes, he did care for her. He knew that much from the hole that formed in his chest each time she left.

He didn't answer.

"I apologize," Andor said.

Stone shrugged. "Like I said, she's fine."

"You made her. I'll defer to you on that."

Another ten minutes passed in silence. Stone counted the seconds, his nerves on edge after Andor's outburst. It had never occurred to him that Vivienne might be in danger. She'd killed those thieves a few days ago and suffered far worse than a swampy village in the name of his experiments. Luring away a scholar should be a trifle.

Yet, they waited.

Twenty minutes after Andor's comment, a giggle bubbled over the water. Stone tensed and monitored the empty stretch of swamp, waiting for someone to round the corner, while Andor hid his hulking form behind the nearest tree. Sure enough, a Lossian couple passed around the farthest pod. Water reached the woman's waist, even though it came only to the man's upper thighs. She laughed again.

Vivienne. Stone recognized the hideous dress. He let out a sigh of relief. In his periphery, Andor studied him. Stone decided not to acknowledge it.

She ran her fingers along the Lossian's neck, and the sucker smiled. He swayed, as if drunk, and the still-disguised Vivienne wrapped her arm around his waist. He leaned on her, and though she stumbled, she held his weight. The Lossian man ran a hand through her black hair and hiccupped.

Udrenit. Stone tensed. He'd never seen a photo of the man, but he trusted Vivienne. Her unaware captive said something in Lossian, the words gurgling like a pot of hot water.

"Ready for that time alone?" she asked in Ethosian. Her grin widened.

The man nodded.

"Over here," she said, pointing toward the edge of the lake.

Stone rested on the balls of his feet, arms tense as he waited for his prey to near. He would only have the element of surprise for at most a second, so he would have to wait until Udrenit came within reach.

The Lossian stumbled and fell into the water with a splash, nearly taking Vivienne with him. Water ricocheted into the air like arrows. She let him fall and stepped back, a barely masked frown breaking the smooth skin on her blue face as the stream pelted her cheeks.

This would do.

While the Lossian eased himself onto his hands and knees, Stone pushed himself to his feet and jumped into the water. The cold liquid stunned him, dragging him toward the lakebed as water pulled on his clothes. The splash caught Udrenit's attention, but Stone extended the barb in his palm and reached for the drunk Lossian's neck before recognition set in. The thorn slipped into the base of Udrenit's spine as it had with each of Stone's victims through the years.

Udrenit's eyes widened, which Stone didn't think was possible for a Lossian face. Camouflaged eyelids pulled back to reveal the Lossian's full eye and the whites hidden along the edges.

But Udrenit didn't fight.

Though most souls struggled, Udrenit left his body almost willingly. Almost no strain pulled on Stone's shoulders as he extracted the man's life force. And as Stone conquered the man's soul, darkness consumed the swamp. The floral musk of the hyacinth flowers dissolved until Stone could smell nothing, see nothing, but the inside of his mind.

Stone retreated inward, pulling Udrenit's soul along with him. The Lossian appeared again, once more on his hands and knees, though no water joined them. As it had with every stolen soul thus far, Udrenit's skin began to gray, and flakes of it fell off here and there. In seconds, the Lossian scholar became a wax figure.

Stone took a deep breath as the rush of knowledge flooded him. He'd gotten better at mastering the theft, and now the memories no longer swarmed him. He could instead scan the soul's information, looking for whatever items of importance he found useful, and come back to the rest later. And this soul contained more information than Stone had ever seen. Contents of whole books swam through his brain, and he even uncovered locations of buried artifacts hidden from the Lossian Blood. Images blurred past of Udrenit browsing the same library again and again, and several titles caught Stone's eye: *The Bond of the Blood, Connected Souls,* and *Ourean Energies.*

Later, Stone would need to do some shopping.

As he prepared to retreat, a memory sparked to life. It flickered, daring him to watch, and a flare of excitement built in his chest without his understanding why. He paused, but ultimately allowed the memory to unfold.

Udrenit knelt before another Lossian seated on a throne in a throne room with walls that glinted like mother of pearl and a ceiling that rounded out several stories above. Four pillars made of brightly-colored coral branched from the corners of the room and arched to meet in the center of the roof. They glowed in greens and reds and blues, casting a kaleidoscope of light across the walls and those walking below. Three polished thrones sat on three separate platforms in the center of the room, each with a set of stairs leading to them.

Another Lossian stood on the stairs leading to the center throne wearing a black shirt and slacks with a black cape fastened with a sapphire at his neck. The fabric glimmered in the brilliant light from above—silk, perhaps. Royalty. This had to be the Blood of Losse.

Stone asked the Lossian's mind for the king's name, and it popped into his mind within seconds: Blood Raften.

A flood of knowledge swirled in the memory, illuminating the scene: this had happened barely a month ago, and Udrenit had been summoned with no explanation as to why. He was merely to find his way to the throne room and to do so quickly. Out of fear, he obliged his king.

Now, Udrenit trembled, though he attempted to hide the shaking by bowing his head. Only the smooth floor appeared in the memory, and Stone grimaced in annoyance. He couldn't study anything with this view.

The swirling knowledge continued, overwhelming Stone's irritation. Scholars like Udrenit were rarely called to the palace to receive positive news. He feared the Blood had qualms with his research, research that had recently come to question whether or not the Blood loyalty could be broken.

Stone smiled, thrilled.

Blood Raften pointed a finger toward Stone—toward Udrenit, really—and leaned forward. "Your research concerns me, scholar."

Udrenit swallowed hard and looked at the floor. The trembling worsened. "D-d-does it, my Blood?"

"Why do you study the blood loyalty with such interest?" the king asked.

"M-mere curiosity, I assure—"

"You will stop," the Blood said.

A powerful jolt ripped through Udrenit's core, and Stone flinched in surprise. The trembling stopped, though Udrenit continued to stare at the tile. Stone expected the man to fall, or to scream, but there was no pain. Instead, Udrenit's head nodded on its own. His body moved without his telling it to.

This had to have been a mandate—a command yakona like Udrenit were unable to resist. In a few words, the Lossian Blood had commanded Udrenit to halt his life's work, and the man had to obey.

Frustration bubbled among the fear in the Lossian's chest. Resentment. Disgust. Disappointment. Stone nodded to himself, understanding this anger. They shared the same hatred.

But Udrenit surprised him.

Instead of resolve, the scholar surrendered to a final

wave of sadness. It consumed him, shoving aside all other emotions. His forehead touched the floor, and tears built in the man's eyes. He gave up. With a direct mandate he could never break, he simply accepted his fate.

A flash of panic blindsided Stone. No wonder Udrenit hadn't fought when Stone stole his soul. The scholar had given up on his research, his joy, and his passion. Without his research, he had nothing left. Life became useless, pointless, and without purpose.

Stone scowled, staring at the Lossian tile with renewed loathing.

The memory faded, and the outside world bled into focus. Stone rubbed his eyes as daylight returned. It took a few moments of blinking, but Udrenit's body finally came into focus. It lay beneath the clear water, face down on the pebbles lining the bottom. Clumps of his skin began to break away, dissolving into dust as all yakona did after death.

"If anything, I did him a favor," Stone said under his breath.

A still-disguised Vivienne winked. Apparently, she hadn't heard him. "Go ahead and change. I think I've earned that beer."

A stranger's blue hand patted Stone's shoulder, and he jumped. A Lossian stood beside him, grinning like that stupid Viking. The man towered over Stone, almost as tall as Andor's natural form.

"Don't do that, Andor," Stone said.

In his Lossian form, Andor chuckled, the sound like a creek falling over rocks. "But it's fun."

Stone frowned and knelt in the pool, tugging the dead Lossian's clothes from his body until nothing but a pair of shorts remained. Since the Lossian had been recently seen, it wouldn't do to wear anything but his most recent wardrobe. More bits of the dead yakona's skin broke away in clumps of dust, swirling with the currents beneath the water. Stone stared, marveling at the unique body composition of the yakona people, until he shook his head and forced himself to focus. It took a few moments of treading through the lake, but he slipped behind a house and tugged on the scholar's sopping wet clothes.

Now changed, Stone closed his eyes, focusing on the shift. Water splashed at his feet, shooting ripples over his clothes. Stone's limbs stretched. Tension built in his head, pressing on his temples. Muscles snapped within him, shifting as he donned his new form. A shiver raced along his back.

When the tension faded, Stone opened his eyes and examined his now-blue hands. He shivered—he hated shifting, as it always left a tickle on the back of his neck —but straightened his shirt and cracked his knuckles. He examined his surroundings, marveling at the wider range of his vision. It was as if his periphery became suddenly sharper, giving him a wider angle on the world than before. Lossian bodies had more for him to study than he imagined.

"Here," Vivienne said from behind him.

He spun around. She leaned against the pod he'd used to hide his change, her palms open and full of the blue hyacinth flowers. He took them and stuffed them in his pockets as she had before she left.

"I'm Elodie," Vivienne said.

"Mosser," Andor shouted from around the corner.

Stone smiled, happy with his newest addition. "And I am Benir Udrenit."

Vivienne grinned.

Andor appeared around the corner. "Did you see a pub on your way in, girl?"

"Several. We need to go to the first one, since I found this guy in another," she said, gesturing to Stone.

"Doesn't matter to me. Stone's buying."

"I'm buying hers, not yours," Stone said.

Vivienne set her hands on her hips. "Oh, behave, you two."

"How well-known was that scholar?" Andor asked.

She looked at Stone. "Very. He'll be addressed by name, so you need to at least try to be pleasant."

He huffed in reply.

"I'm serious," she pressed.

"Fine, fine," Stone said, batting away the comment with a flick of his wrist.

She poked his arm. "You can't be gruff or rude, and

if I tell you to flirt with me, then do it. He couldn't keep his hands off of me in that other bar."

Andor chuckled, but Stone pursed his lips. "If I must."

She scoffed. "I'm quite a catch, thank you."

"She is," Andor said with a nod.

Vivienne nodded in apparent thanks with a graceful bow of her head.

"Children," Stone said under his breath.

"Behave," she reminded him.

"Yes, yes. I will."

They rounded the bend at the end of the waterway and took the open lane to their left. Vivienne pointed to one of the identical pods. "Here, this is it."

"How on Earth can you tell?" Stone asked.

"The markings by the door."

Stone studied the front entrance, and sure enough, three black lines had been painted on the right-hand side of the hole that served as a door.

They entered, and all light faded to the barest glow. Candles sat in glass bowls attached to the ceilings with hooks. Orange light glinted off ripples in the water without lighting the surface beneath. Stone's bare feet glided along the pebbles, and slime coated the rocks in the tavern. His toes curled in disgust, but he tried his best to keep his opinion of the pub from reaching his face.

A Lossian man sat in the farthest corner, hunched

over a white cup filled with brown liquid. He didn't glance up as they entered, and instead kept his eyes on the cup before him.

Vivienne sat at a table by the door, and Andor followed suit. Stone joined them, perching on the small, white stool made from the same material as the table and building around them. At least these were resourceful people, reusing a material they apparently had in abundant supply.

A young, Lossian woman walked out of a nearby room, her feet barely causing ripples as she walked. "What can I get you?"

Lossian—she'd spoken Lossian, and Stone understood. He took a deep breath, content with all he'd gathered from this scholar.

Vivienne held up three fingers. "Beers, please."

The waitress nodded and disappeared back into the other room.

"Care to tell us of your research?" Andor asked Stone.

Stone stared at the disguised Andor, mouth parted slightly in surprise. He couldn't know what their trip to Adenot was truly about. He couldn't understand what Stone was trying to do, not Andor. He was muscle, a loyal servant to a man Stone hated. He rarely thought ahead on the simplest of missions.

Vivienne pinched her eyebrows and pouted her lips, the expression confusing enough to distract Stone from his panic. She stared at him as if she were trying to point out something important but was unable to speak.

"Say something!" she mouthed wordlessly.

Oh. She was trying to break his dread and get him to focus.

Of course, Andor didn't know. He couldn't. He'd meant for Stone to discuss the Lossian's research, not his own. Andor had addressed Stone as the Lossian scholar, as they were supposed to.

"It's quite dull," Stone finally said with a wave of his hand, hoping he'd covered his momentary blunder. But Andor squinted and set his elbows on the table, leaning forward in what could only be suspicion.

Vivienne eyed Stone but ultimately smiled and nudged Andor's side. "Mosser, darling, tell me about your latest adventure."

Andor leaned back and crossed his arms without taking his eyes from Stone. "What do you want to know, Elodie?"

"Everything!" she said, her grin widening.

Andor smirked and relaxed his shoulders. "Don't you have plenty of adventures yourself?"

"None as interesting as yours. I've heard stories and absolutely must know if they're true."

Using flattery to distract Andor— Stone almost nodded with approval. Smart girl.

The young waitress brought three white cups and

set them on the table without a word before disappearing once more into the other room. Andor grabbed two and handed one to Vivienne. Stone grabbed the remaining cup and sipped it.

Sludge slid down his throat, so thick it seemed almost like the slime coating his feet. He gagged, and Andor laughed.

Stone shook his head to get the taste out of his mouth. "I can see why you were surprised to hear we wanted these."

"They're truly disgusting," Andor said. He tossed his head back and downed his in a single gulp.

"Why are you drinking it, then?" Stone asked.

Vivienne mimicked the Viking and downed hers in a single swig. "They will knock you on your rump, that's why. They can make you forget any pain in the world."

"Three more!" Andor roared.

Their lone companion in the room glanced up from his cup, and the clink of mugs in the other room answered Andor's command.

Stone pushed his toward the Viking. "All yours."

Andor shrugged. "Suit yourself."

"I want to hear about an adventure," Vivienne said again.

"Right, of course, little princess," Andor said. He grinned in response to Vivienne's wide smile, and for a moment, Stone's hand tightened into a fist. He didn't want her to look at him that way, even if it was merely a ploy to divert his attention from Stone's blunder.

He tensed his jaw and occupied himself by looking out the window. He would thank her later for distracting him but remind her not to be so openly flirtatious. It would give away her deception if she overdid it. At least she had picked up on his silent cue to keep the Viking busy.

For now, Stone would rummage through the scholar's memories and discover what they'd come for: Benir's home, which would likely contain the artifacts and books that might be Stone's key to breaking his connection to Niccoli for good.

After Andor had wasted two hours and plenty of Stone's perfectly good money on terrible Lossian beer, Stone finally stood inside Udrenit's home not far from where Stone had stolen the man's soul. The scholar's savings were stashed in the bookcase on the second floor, which served him well as the same bookcases housed most of the books he intended to steal.

"Hurry up and get the man's money, will you?" Andor asked. He crossed his arms and leaned against the door, head swaying as he stared into the water at his feet.

Vivienne hiccupped and covered her mouth with her thin, blue fingers. She leaned against the wall beside him. Her head tilted and rested on the Viking's chest. Stone paused, fists once more clenching. Andor patted her shoulder, but she burped. Both burst into giggles.

Stone grimaced. Drunkards.

He began up the white steps, trailing water as he left the swamp to the first floor. Trails of slime marked the scholar's well-worn path up the stairs and through a short hallway that ended in an arch.

Stone paused in the doorframe to take in the man's library. Bookshelves covered every wall and spanned past him into wings on either side of the hall. It seemed the entire second floor was devoted to bookcases, each of which was filled with books. Stone took a deep breath and leaned against the doorframe, hand over his heart as he took in the beautiful sight. He wished he could take each and every one—the fools who inherited the house would likely use them for firewood when they realized Udrenit was gone—but he couldn't. As hard as it was, he had to focus. He'd come for specific books he'd uncovered in the scholar's memories over the two hours he'd had to listen to Andor ramble at the tavern. Those he could likely hide in his waistband. Any others would arouse suspicion. At most, he could take four or five others and forfeit those to Niccoli's library to read later.

Stone tore through the library, heading first for the silver in the second cupboard. After that, he grabbed eight books: four related to the Blood Loyalty and four on creature lore.

"I'm hungry!" Andor roared from the first floor.

Vivienne said something Stone couldn't hear. She and the Viking burst once more into giggles.

Stone grimaced and shook his head in annoyance. Bloody nuisance of a Viking.

He tucked the thin books into his waistline and wrapped his arm around the others, careful to keep them high enough that they wouldn't get wet as he left. By leaning his arm against the outlines under his clothes, he could keep them in place. He muttered a silent prayer that those hidden in his pants would remain hidden when he shifted. He'd learned his lesson from the day he met Death the first time. Hopefully, Niccoli hadn't.

13

THREATS

August, 967 A.D.
Niccoli's Guild

It took several hours, followed by a pause to shift into their natural forms and dry their clothes, but Stone eventually joined Vivienne and Andor at the entrance to Niccoli's guild. The lilac bushes had grown over the last six decades, and they rose a good five feet from the dirt. Heat faded from Stone's back as he passed through the entrance, and the shade came as a welcome reprieve from the sun. He wiped away sweat from his brow, but his upward glance revealed a distinct lack of guards in the branches overhead.

"Where did they go?" Vivienne asked, head tilted back to examine the canopy.

Andor frowned, the numbness of his drinking

apparently fading. He drew his sword and kept the blade pointed forward as they continued their walk. Stone didn't bother drawing his. As he was so often reminded by the isen he loathed, it served more as decoration.

Minutes passed in silence until a laugh came from farther down the path. The hum of conversation bubbled as they neared, and within seconds, the laughter of a crowd filled the once-quiet entrance.

Past the final bend in the path, isen filled the primary clearing of Niccoli's guild. A thousand of them at least, all of whom carried metal plates of food. Slaves, marked as always by their beige pants, walked by carrying trays of hams and cheeses, others with breads or silver flagons that revealed wine as they were poured into goblets.

Stone paused at the opening, brows furrowed in confusion. He could barely hear himself think, despite the massive space in which he stood. He wished for something to cover his ears—anything to block out the sheer volume of voices.

Good lord, he hated people.

One young woman in beige slacks stopped in front of him and bowed her head, lifting a tray of sliced ham to his face. She kept her eyes on the ground, and her blond hair spilled over pale shoulders and a stained shirt that was likely the only one she owned.

"Finally!" Andor said. He grabbed four slices of the

dead animal and continued toward the manor. Stone brushed by the slave without a word, assuming Vivienne would follow. The beacon burning in his chest revealed that she paused by the slave but ultimately joined him.

He pushed past those in his way, and though a few shot glares toward him, he couldn't care less. If they didn't want to be jostled, they'd leave a path to the mansion for others to take. He needed to hide the books in his pants lining, and the crowd would likely serve as a suitable distraction provided they didn't knock him over.

"What's all this for?" Vivienne asked, her voice barely audible in the clamor.

Stone didn't answer. He wouldn't waste his breath, not in this noise. He had no idea, anyway, as Niccoli had never once hosted any such event in his time with the isen master. The sudden swell of activity bothered Stone. Whenever Niccoli surprised him, bad news followed without fail.

Andor disappeared into the crowd, his assignment apparently complete, but Stone continued toward the manor. Though several bodies forced him to take detours, he reached the front door in a matter of minutes. Sweat beaded along his neck as the books in his pants lining slipped with each step. He took the stairs with careful steps, a hand on his waistband. One slid farther down his leg than the rest, but he gritted his teeth and pressed onward. Even if it fell, he could likely pick it up without being noticed in the throng.

"May I?" Vivienne asked from behind him. He turned to see her pointing toward a passing tray of pineapple slices.

He nodded. She smiled and disappeared into the crowd.

Stone pressed onward and shoved open the front door, tension building in his shoulders as he fought the impulse to run up the stairs. Bodies lingered in the hallway, blocking his route, but he forced his way through the throng, up the stairs, and into his bedroom with barely a breath. It wasn't until he sat on his bed that he could suck in the air his body so desperately needed.

He wasted no time in loosening the lining of his pants. The books fell to the floor, and he scooped them into his hands. He pried away the floorboard that held his forbidden treasures and piled them inside.

Someone knocked at the door.

He froze, shoulders straining as he fought to control his panic, but slowly replaced the floorboard. All evidence of his secret now hidden, he cleared his throat. "I don't want to be bothered!"

The door opened, and Stone rose on impulse to belay suspicion. He chewed his lip and glowered at the entrance, ready to snap at whoever waited on the other side. No one should open his door without announcing themselves, except of course for Vivienne or—

Niccoli stood in the doorway, arms crossed. He smirked, and it took everything Stone had to not swallow hard in response to his master's sudden appearance. He relaxed his shoulders, but barely.

"I assume you noticed the celebration," Niccoli said.

Stone nodded, his neck so tense it cracked.

"Then why are you here?"

"I hate crowds," Stone answered. It was the truth, in a way.

"Join me," Niccoli said.

Stone hesitated but ultimately obeyed. They entered the hall, and Stone closed his door behind them. His jaw ached from his nerves, but he needed to contain himself. He'd nearly given himself away to Andor earlier. Niccoli would not so easily overlook stupid mistakes.

"What are we celebrating?" Stone asked as their boots clomped down the stairs.

"I now have the largest guild in Ourea," Niccoli answered.

Stone's eyebrows raised in surprise. "How do you know?"

"My only competitor was killed in a scuffle while fighting for a family of unawaken isen discovered in Spain. Four major guilds were destroyed or disbanded in a single fight. To think, I would have been there if not for your advice. You may have saved my life, Stone."

Tension returned to Stone's shoulders, and he forced himself to keep his eyes ahead instead of grimacing as he so badly wanted to. He'd missed an opportunity to kill Niccoli after all. The thought caused a flicker of pain in his gut. Elsewhere, isen with less foresight to warn their master away from Spain were now free, while Stone continued to serve Niccoli.

His master turned and gave him a smile, but the slight glare in the man's eye told another story. He knew. He knew Stone hated him. He knew he'd dodged a second encounter with Death and had Stone to thank. He was merely rubbing salt in the wound.

Stone finally nodded. "I'm sure you're pleased."

"Quite pleased."

Niccoli led them around a corner and into the library. Only the books on the higher shelves could be seen over the sea of heads filling the room. The sofas and chairs had been pushed against the wall for extra space, and the fireplace sat dormant in the summer heat.

The beacon in Stone's chest flickered. He spun, and Vivienne's dark eyes caught his from across the room as he entered. She smiled, her dark curls now loose around her pale face as she chatted with a young man whose name Stone hadn't bothered to learn. The boy grinned and leaned closer to Vivienne, his focus shifting to her chest.

Stone clenched a fist, but Niccoli set a hand on his shoulder and tightened his grip to a painful degree. Stone grimaced, his knees dipping from the pain. He bit the inside of his cheek to hide his expression, but he knew better than to think Niccoli had fetched him to say hello. He hadn't come merely to drag Stone to a party. Niccoli had come to make a point, and Stone was about to discover exactly what his master wanted to impress upon him.

The isen master leaned in, his nails still digging into Stone's shoulder. "How are your experiments going?"

"Well," Stone said, gritting his teeth through the pain.

"Do you know why I haven't asked what you're studying?"

Stone didn't answer.

Niccoli continued regardless. "Because your experiments with that girl of yours don't matter. No matter what you're looking for, no matter what you're doing, you will not escape me. I own you, boy, same as the first day we met. I always will. No book, no soul, no experiment can save you. I'd sooner kill you than set you free."

His grip tightened, and Stone rested a hand against the wall for support as he was forced to lean even closer to his master.

Niccoli set his mouth near Stone's ear. "Do you still want to continue these experiments, even if they don't matter?"

Stone fought back the tears of pain pooling in his eyes. "Yes."

"Then you will never leave my presence again."

Stone hesitated, but there was nothing he could do. Nothing he could say would change the outcome of this conversation.

He nodded.

"Do you understand what will happen if you disobey?" Niccoli asked.

Stone caught his master's eye. The man grinned, a snarl that etched lines into his face. He lowered his head, and shadows from his brow hid his eyes.

"I don't," Stone admitted.

Niccoli released his grip on Stone's shoulder. Stone sighed with relief, but the man grabbed his collar. Stone flew forward, now inches from his master's face as the old isen spoke. "If you ever leave my presence again, I will end your experiments forever and chain you for the rest of your life. I would tear your room to kindling and burn everything you may have been hiding from me. And most of all, I would get rid of your means to experiment. I prefer not to kill my own children or grandchildren, Stone, but I feel I need to make this clear. I need you. I do not need her."

With a nod toward Vivienne, Niccoli made his

threat abundantly clear. A flicker of fear burned in Stone's chest alongside the beacon he associated with Vivienne.

As if she'd heard her name, Vivienne glanced at him again, still grinning. Her eyes shifted to Niccoli, and she quickly looked away. Her shoulders hunched a bit, and she kept her gaze rooted on the plate in her hands. Whatever she'd seen in Niccoli's face had scared the smile from hers.

Niccoli continued. "If you continue to make life difficult for me, if you lie to me again, I will end you. I have run out of patience with you, boy, and this is your final chance."

The grip on Stone's collar disappeared, and he stumbled against the wall as he regained his balance. Niccoli left, but Stone didn't follow to see which direction he'd taken. He rubbed his shoulder, frozen in place as he fought to process this new threat. The scholar's ultimatum made more sense, now, and Stone realized that he, too, had been given the final choice: obey or die.

Without a word, he returned to his room. He barely noticed the stairs or the crowds and, before long, sat once more on his bed. He held his sword in his hand as he had so many times in recent years, wondering yet again if he had the strength to end himself.

How hopeless. Niccoli knew he planned to leave. He knew Stone hated his life in the guild. And most of all, Niccoli seemed convinced there was no way for Stone to escape. His unwavering certainty washed all hope from Stone's plans. Despite his successful theft today, even he doubted breaking the bond was even possible after sorting through the scholar's memories. A few books from a scholar's library wouldn't free him. He'd been a fool, an idiot even, to hope so fiercely. To wish. He was a scientist, a logical man. He couldn't hope and wish. Such luxuries were reserved for children.

He lifted the sword tip and studied it. He lost either way. If he saw Death again of his own doing, Niccoli would likely send Vivienne right after. He would kill her out of spite. And as much as Stone hated to admit it, he wouldn't let that happen to her.

With a frustrated scream, he threw the sword across the room. It clanged with all the anger burning in his chest and smacked against the wall with a thud. He hated her, in that moment—hated her for stealing what little freedom he had. She served as his weakness, something Niccoli could dangle over a pit and use to coerce him into obedience. Stone had always survived without caring, and he hated that blasted French-woman for taking his final freedom from him.

He lay on the bed, mud streaking across his blanket as he smacked his boots against the mattress. His cheeks burned, likely flushed with anger, and loose strands of his hair filled his periphery.

Your freedom! Hmph! What about mine? a voice in his head shouted.

He paused, brows twisted in confusion. Who—

Who were you to steal my soul? From where I stand, you're the enslaver. I'm the slave. It's only right you should feel this, too.

The scholar, Udrenit, had finally found his voice.

Stone bristled and sat upright. The nerve. *I do what I must to survive. You were convenient.*

You hypocritical—

Stone interrupted. *I know what I did. I realize the hypocrisy, and I did what I needed to survive. I will not apologize. Besides, you'd given up. What life did you have left to live?*

The scholar didn't answer.

That's what I thought. Stone stood and kicked the wall with the full brunt of his anger. The wood creaked with the threat of splintering but didn't break. He kicked again and again, but the wood barely budged beneath his foot. He kicked until his muscles ached and forced him to sink to the floor. He sat with his arms draped over his knees, staring at the dent he'd made in his own wall. Pathetic—he wasn't even strong enough to break wood.

He dug his hands into his hair and grunted in frustration, but he couldn't shake the truth in the scholar's words. He truly had enslaved every soul he'd stolen. They all obeyed him, gave him their memories, skills, and appearance without question, and not out of kindness. He used them like a master used his slaves, and he was no better than the manor lord who had enslaved him since birth. He was no better than Niccoli. But his freedom mattered most. It always would.

And yet...

He stared at the floor, his thoughts drifting to Vivienne.

The door opened and closed without a knock. The beacon in his chest burned at her proximity, but he didn't react. Her boot heels clacked against the wood, heading for him. She knelt and set a hand in his hair. Stone leaned away, refusing to look up, and she pulled her hand away. She sat with her back to the nearest wall.

"What did Niccoli say to you?" she asked.

Stone shook his head in answer, slowly at first, but the motion quickened with each beat of his heart. He finally held his hands to his ears and forced it to stop.

She set a hand on his ankle, and he allowed it.

"We can beat him," she said.

"How?" he asked, still staring at the floor.

"I don't know. You're the smart one."

She chuckled, but Stone didn't indulge her. A few words didn't change facts. He had no way out, no revelation from the scholar's work. Nothing. At this point, escape would take a miracle. He could only wait for an opportune moment to find him. A bitter thought reminded him of his last attempt at hope and how utterly it had failed him, but he forced himself to shake it away.

Perhaps, an opportunity would find him. In the meantime, he would be the errand boy Niccoli needed and curse every day that passed as he awaited his one chance to leave.

14

THE FAVOR

April, 991 A.D.
Niccoli's Guild

Stone's sword lay on the floor where he'd thrown it twenty-four years ago during his tantrum over Niccoli's threat to kill Vivienne. He feared picking it up would inspire him to use it on himself, so he left it on the floorboards.

Tonight, he sat on his bed, legs crossed as he stared up at moonlight drifting through the hole in the canopy. He lost himself in thought.

So many wasted years. He counted time as it passed by him, though he began to doubt why it was important. He now looked to be in his early twenties, as he'd skipped a year or two between souls. Nothing major. He'd survive. But the scholar's outburst had stuck with him, and he stole only when required for his own youth. One day, he would discover a way to live without stealing souls. For now, they would have to forgive his slavery. And for whatever reason, they all did in the end. After Udrenit had forced his way through Stone's mind, the floodgates opened. The voices clamored for his attention, buzzing like flies in his ear. Even Udrenit wanted to speak with him nowadays, and that he often allowed in an attempt to better understand the Blood Loyalty. Thus far, however, that had served no use. Udrenit had never come close to breaking the loyalty; he was apparently the first to merely suggest it was possible.

A sudden urgency filled Stone, compelling him to walk downstairs. It came without rational thought or reason, but the sensation all but dragged him down the hallway. He sighed. Niccoli must have wanted him for something, likely another fruitless unawaken isen hunt. They didn't seem to exist anymore, and the last six hunts had turned up nothing.

Still, Stone obeyed. He ambled down the hall and took the stairs at his own pace. He had to obey, but he would keep his master waiting as long as possible. He trailed his finger along the paneled walls, his fingertip dipping as each panel ended. When he finally arrived at the study door, he opened it without waiting for an invitation. Technically, he'd already received one.

Niccoli sat at his desk, elbows on the surface while

he stared into a book. He didn't look up as Stone entered or acknowledge the click of the latch as it closed.

"I have a favor to ask, one that has been troubling me for decades," Niccoli said.

Stone raised an eyebrow in curiosity. A favor—that couldn't be good. "What is it?"

"Do you know why I've built such a massive guild?"

Greed, likely. Stone didn't answer.

"I need strength in numbers to overthrow my own master and take my rightful place as Ourea's most powerful isen, Stone. It's time. We haven't found any fresh recruits to turn, and the guild won't get much larger at this point. I need you to help me plan my attack and kill my master."

Stone's mouth fell open, and for a moment, he couldn't speak.

"I didn't know betraying a master was an option," he finally said.

Niccoli's eyes narrowed. "It isn't an option for you. You don't have a guild to support you, and even if I let you build one, yours would never rival mine."

Stone almost laughed. What a fool. Niccoli likely feared Stone doing to him what he'd apparently always wanted to do to his own master. The idiot. It was almost as if the man never suspected what Stone thought was painfully obvious all along: that Stone wanted only knowledge, isolation, and freedom.

Niccoli continued. "In exchange for your assistance, I will give you your precious book."

Stone's eyebrows rose, and Niccoli nodded as if he knew he'd hit a nerve. The idiot. Stone's copy of *the Anglo-Saxon Chronicles* would have been suitable leverage for a smaller matter, but escape mattered more.

"You've behaved yourself, Stone. I believe you've changed, and I'm giving you this opportunity to prove yourself. Up until now, I haven't mentioned it because I didn't want to give you ideas, but I can't figure out how to do this. I've tried to plan this for years, but nothing I've devised will work. I only get one chance at this, and I need your input. But I'll make assurances that, if you get me killed, you and that girl of yours will be killed as well."

"Vivienne."

"What?"

"Never mind. Tell me about your master." Stone could guess what Niccoli's assurances would be. He would likely keep an eye on Vivienne and assign one of his trusted isen to keep an eye on her. She would have to kill or elude them, but Stone would factor it into his plan.

"You'll help?" Niccoli asked.

"I want my book," he lied. "Besides, I don't have a choice, do I?"

"If you betray me—"

"Death and mayhem, et cetera. I know. On with it."

Niccoli examined Stone in silence, and it was all Stone could do to not burst into a grin. His chest burned with joy—true joy, the first he'd experienced in decades. He couldn't believe it. He even dared to hope that this would be his chance, the one chance to escape. He would not miss this opening in Niccoli's armor as he had missed the opportunity in Spain.

He held his breath, fighting his excitement as he kept a neutral expression. He focused on his brow, furrowing it to hide his smile. He didn't dare clear his throat, but he did clench his hands a little tighter on the edge of the table to relieve the tension.

Niccoli reached into a drawer in the desk and pulled out a piece of parchment. He unfolded it to reveal a map covered with seven, glowing, green stars much like the blue triangles on the map Vivienne had given him of the township of Adenot. Forests covered most of the map, and houses were littered across the paper. In the center, a massive home appeared, almost ten times the size of the others.

"Is this to scale?" Stone asked, tapping the center house.

Niccoli nodded.

Stone shook his head in annoyance. The mansion must have been four times larger than Niccoli's, which meant complications and hidden rooms. Stone studied the map, looking closer at any line that stood out. He discovered smaller homes outlined with dots rather than lines. "And these?"

"Houses built in the trees. What this map doesn't show is the sheer size of this forest. There is no gap to the sky. It's all canopy and underbrush except for a few, well-worn, heavily guarded paths."

Fire. Burn them out, Stone thought. He held his tongue.

Niccoli tapped the map. "My master, Bakit, lives in a warm region of Ourea far from any yakona kingdoms or cities. I lived there for a time, and he uses these seven lichgates to bring the souls and resources he needs. They form a circle around his home. Though it opens him up to attack from all angles, the paths are guarded, and he can always escape through one of them if forced. He has clear exits and likely knows them all by heart."

"What does he do if someone trespasses?"

"They disappear."

Stone nodded. Evidently, Bakit didn't hesitate.

Niccoli sat down and rubbed his face. "To make this harder, his guards all steal Hillsidian souls, which are the best trackers in Ourea. They have the greatest sense of stealth and speed imaginable. Even when he's expecting company, they're on high alert."

Stone rubbed his chin. It seemed he could benefit from a Hillsidian soul. If this turned out in his favor, he would likely have to break his oath to steal a soul every decade and find a Hillsidian before his ten years were up.

"What is the layout of the house?" Stone asked.

"A labyrinth. He adds onto it every year, constantly building new hallways and additions. He moves his room every five years or so to keep things interesting."

Stone rummaged through the information he'd gathered, but it wasn't enough for a plan. Not yet. There were too many moving parts to plan around. "Can we visit beforehand? I want to see the layout for myself and—"

Niccoli shook his head. "It would arouse suspicion. When you're planning something, you're too obvious about it. Why do you think I've always kept such a close eye on you?"

Stone frowned in response.

The isen master lifted a single finger and waved it in Stone's face. "I have one opportunity and only one. Everything must be planned before we arrive."

"Fine. What does Bakit think of you?"

"He monitors me carefully. I'm the lone threat to his empire. I began hiding some of my newer isen families out of reach, farther than I believe he can sense them. It has helped quell his suspicion, but not by much."

Stone stared at the map, but he stopped listening. Niccoli had betrayed crucial information—that he couldn't tell how far Bakit could sense Niccoli's isen, but also that there was clearly a range. It was confirmation that Niccoli himself would misplace isen if they were far enough away.

Stone gripped the edge of the desk to steady himself and plowed ahead. "Would you be able to give Bakit gifts of any kind? Would he suspect poisoning?"

Niccoli tapped his cheek, quiet for a moment before answering. "He expects tribute when I do visit. If I were to bring something truly unique, he would take it. He would test it on someone else first, but if they didn't die, he would eat it, too."

"Do you have any reason to visit him?"

"In a few years, yes. It will be my two-hundredth year of serving him. He will expect a gift." Niccoli added the last sentence with a grimace.

"How many years?"

"Three."

Stone nodded. "I need to study this map and sketch out ideas. May I have it and a journal?"

Niccoli hesitated, eyes narrowing once more as he studied Stone, but Stone didn't budge. He needed both of those things if there was any hope of success, and it was not out of bounds to ask.

"Very well. Here." Niccoli reached into a desk drawer and pulled out a journal bound in leather.

Stone hoped it would have notes of Niccoli's in them but knew better. He likely had a collection of empty journals on hand.

"I expect that back when you're done," Niccoli said with a glance toward the blank book.

"Of course," Stone said, shoulders tensing with aggravation as he spoke.

He left the room without another word, map and journal under his arm. Once out in the hall, he allowed himself a smirk. It was the perfect opportunity. During the attack, he would slip away. He would lose his book, but he would be forever free if only he could figure out how to distract Niccoli long enough to make it happen.

15

THE PLAN

April, 991 A.D.
Niccoli's Guild

For several days after his meeting with Niccoli, Stone barely slept. He pored over the maps in his possession, studying Niccoli's most of all. The seven lichgates surrounding Bakit's camp all led somewhere, and one of them must contain a path of lichgates that would take him far, far away. He resolved to have Vivienne test them, as she had an uncanny way of avoiding trouble. Or finding it. He couldn't quite tell with her.

The musk of aged paper and spilled ink hung in the room like a fog. Parchment covered his floor. Piles of maps and ripped pages from the blank journal Niccoli had given him created an ocean of notes that barred any exit from the room. Stone didn't mind, as each pile contained a theory on how to best execute Bakit and escape in the process.

Stone moved between the piles, paper crunching under his toes as he carried Niccoli's map with him and weighed his options. Map after map passed under his nose as he searched for any that might connect with Niccoli's.

After three days of searching, one of the maps finally sparked a sense of familiarity. A few houses drawn on one of Vivienne's maps bore a striking resemblance to those on Niccoli's. Stone pressed them side by side and matched their angles until—yes! Vivienne's map of a distant valley matched perfectly with Niccoli's top left corner.

He'd found a way to escape.

Relief crashed through him like a wave. He inhaled, savoring the rush. He leaned against his bed and rubbed his face, not quite believing he'd found a clear path out of Bakit's manor. But thanks to Vivienne's near-century of exploration, he had maps of this area, maps even Niccoli might not possess.

Focus. He needed to focus.

Stone traced his finger over Vivienne's map, following a series of lichgates out of Bakit's camp and through fields and countryside alike. Her route took him twelve lichgates away from Bakit's camp, and if her notes were accurate, three of the twelve were difficult to find. Stone could hide them further during his escape to make tracking him impossible, but he would need to first steal a Hillsidian soul to help him with his stealth. He couldn't afford to be tracked at all.

He laughed in surprise, almost unable to believe he'd devised an escape. His stomach gurgled, and he looked around for the plate of food he'd brought up yesterday. It sat on the bed, and a fly landed on a hunk of half-eaten bread. A bit of crust broke off as the bug landed, settling like dust on the plate.

Stone grimaced. He didn't want to leave, but he would probably have to go for food soon. For the moment, he pressed on.

He returned to the maps and ran his finger along the path again. He wouldn't draw out his route for fear Niccoli would find his collection. Instead, he would memorize it, running the path in his mind each night until the fateful day he could finally escape.

Beautiful. Stone now had a plan to escape and, he believed, a suitable way to distract Niccoli long enough for him to leave. But if only—

The door creaked open.

"Shoo, go. I'm busy," he said without looking up.

A woman cursed in French. He lifted his head to find Vivienne in the doorframe, one hand on her heart as she eyed the floor. The door swept aside papers as she fought to enter.

"Oh, good!" Stone jumped to his feet. Maps fluttered from his hands and sailed to the floor. He almost couldn't believe he'd missed her beacon as she'd neared, but he had been so consumed by his work and as distracted as he hoped to make Niccoli.

"What in Heaven's name…" she didn't finish the thought and instead trailed her eyes over the stale hunk of bread sitting on his mattress.

"I have a lot for you to do. Here," Stone shoved the half-rotted food to the floor, and the metal plate smacked against one of the many piles. He patted the bed and took a seat but stood almost as quickly. He needed to find the maps he'd dropped if he was to tell her his plan.

She pinched her nose. "You smell like a horse stall. I'm not sitting next to you until you've had a bath. When did you last leave this room?"

"Don't be ridiculous. I don't have time for baths. Here, listen—close the door. Why are you standing there?"

She chuckled, hand still on her chest, but finally obeyed. "I don't think I've ever seen you this excited before. What's going on?"

"I know how to escape."

Her smile faded, and she stood a little taller. "Tell me."

Stone tapped his fingers on the mattress, waiting for Vivienne to say something. She sat on his bed, eyebrows pinched as she took in everything he'd said. She was no doubt searching for holes in his theories, but he'd become quite certain there weren't any.

"Tell me again," she said.

He released a huff of annoyance but repeated himself regardless. "You begin moving all of my maps, journals, and books—anything I've hidden here—to the abandoned house you found here." He pointed to one of her maps, finger hovering on a square she'd drawn into a remote countryside. It was an Ourean house, built on a farm left vacant for centuries. Legends and rumors abounded around it, many claiming it was haunted by the family murdered there. Stone didn't care. He needed a new home in Ourea, and he could use the rumors to keep out trespassers. In his research, he'd discovered it was easier to sense Vivienne over great distances in Earth than Ourea, so he wanted to remain in Ourea if possible.

"In the meantime, we both steal Hillsidian souls," Vivienne added.

He nodded, glad she'd at least been listening when he shared this idea the first time. "To celebrate Niccoli's two hundred years with Bakit, we will make two hundred barrels of poisoned wine as tribute. While you find us Hillsidian souls, I'll begin making wine poisoned with mandragora and use that as the tribute to Bakit, using only enough mandragora to make everyone slowly fall asleep as they drink it."

"How much will it take?" she asked.

"I need to take some measurements, but we'll need one glass of wine per person to send them to sleep. It should take an hour at most for any drinker to fall asleep in his seat."

She rubbed her hands together. "Two months before we leave, I'll talk to the slaves in this guild and organize a rebellion to take place while the isen are unconscious in Bakit's mansion. Since Niccoli will need slaves to help serve the wine and will probably use them as tribute, he'll bring enough of them to cause trouble."

Stone set his hands on her shoulders and caught her eye. "You must be quiet and never let anyone realize that the slave rebellion is coming from you. We only get this one chance. Niccoli cannot know about the rebellion."

"But he'll know about the poisoned wine."

Stone nodded. "He will think that's the full plan— use the wine to put Bakit to sleep so that Niccoli can kill him where he falls. With most of Bakit's isen asleep, Niccoli will then be able to escape. He doesn't know we'll have a rebellion to distract him long enough for me to run."

"Are you sure you don't want me there?" she asked.

"You should wait for me at the abandoned house." Stone studied his hands to resist the impulse to betray why he wanted her out of the fray. She was leverage that could be used against him. If she were there, she could ruin everything.

Vivienne paused, and her eyes shifted out of focus as if she'd had an idea. She brushed her thin fingers along her jawline, and Stone watched her, waiting for the inevitable comment. Her eyes darted over the maps at their feet, resting on one of the piles he'd dismissed as useless.

Eventually, she shrugged. "Very well."

"What is it?" he asked, brow wrinkling with distrust.

She frowned. "Nothing. This is a good plan."

"No, what were you debating?" he asked. She'd settled on something, he knew it. She'd decided to do something and now wouldn't tell him what. She gravitated toward trouble, and he needed to know she would listen.

"Nothing. It's unimportant," she said with a flick of her wrist.

"Don't go to Bakit's. Do you understand?"

She paused, eyes on him. She smirked, but her eyes narrowed. "I understand."

He nodded—that was that—and continued. "When most of the room is asleep, I will indicate to a slave of your choosing that the rebellion should begin. He can then start the ruckus while Niccoli is consumed with trying to kill Bakit. The rebellion should light the woods and everything in it on fire. That will create enough of a distraction for me to slip away."

Vivienne bit her lip and stared at the piles on the floor. "A lot could go wrong with this plan."

"It will work."

"You're sure?"

Stone nodded, though a flicker of doubt burned in his chest. Yes, this plan relied on others more than he'd like. Yes, it meant standing in the middle of a warzone before he could escape. And yes, it meant evading skilled guards who killed without pause when he could barely lift a sword in a fight. Worse yet, he'd been under Niccoli's control so long, he almost couldn't imagine being free. It had always been a dream barely out of his reach, but to finally taste it …

… he wouldn't let this fail. This was the first real chance he'd ever gotten. He couldn't waste it.

"How much time do we have?" she asked.

"Three years."

She stood. "Well, let's prepare, then. I believe we both have some work to do."

16

ATTACK

July, 994 A.D.
Traveling in Ourea

For three years, Stone implemented every facet of his plan. And for three years, he waited with tense joy for the day he would finally be able to leave Niccoli forever.

Today was that day.

Stone crossed the final lichgate into Bakit's territory. Blue light assaulted his peripheral vision. His stomach churned. Nausea shot into his cheeks, but he swallowed hard to suppress it. He didn't dare bend over to catch his breath. His nerves already assaulted him, burning his fingertips as he monitored the trees for guards. The woods on this side of the portal held thick trunks and vines, with a canopy so think he couldn't see the sun. Instead, lanterns filled with candles illuminated the path, casting shadows between the trees.

Horses snorted to his left as they, too, passed through the lichgate. Four bay mares pulled one of the four carts full of poisoned wine, their hooves clopping along the soil without rhythm. It creaked and swayed with each rotation of the wooden wheels, but the barrels had been tied to the frame with more than enough rope. He trudged along the dirt path beside the horses, the wide road still offering another four feet of space for him to walk. Niccoli's isen choked every inch of space behind him, a small army with no idea of what was to come. Niccoli hadn't shared any details for fear of the ruse spreading and, between the slave rebellion and Bakit's isen discovering what Niccoli had done, Stone suspected many of these men would not survive the night.

The slaves trailed at the end of the convoy, most of them ready to rebel with a single nod from Stone. They'd had enough of Niccoli, same as him. Tonight would be a night of retribution for some and freedom for others.

Stone gripped the hilt of his sword for comfort. His cheeks flushed with the desire to vomit as nerves played with his stomach. In a matter of hours, three years of planning would either come to fruition or unravel before his eyes.

As long as Stone got away, he didn't care what happened.

The road passed beneath tree after tree with barely a break in the canopy to let in sun, and bramble bushes lined the road, barring any exit from the path. Stone spotted various rope bridges and guards in the branches thanks to the Hillsidian soul Vivienne had brought back to the guild for him. Niccoli had allowed it, as Stone had convinced him it was crucial to his plan's success, and he marveled at the soul's skill. It alerted him to the barest snap of a twig or groan of a branch as a soldier's weight pressed into it. He often wondered how Vivienne had managed to subdue such a powerful tracker, much less drag him back to the guild for Stone to absorb. Well, he had theories, but he didn't like to pursue them. She did what she had to, and only that mattered.

Soon, Stone would be free, and Vivienne would no longer be Niccoli's leverage against him.

Footsteps padded along the soil behind him, alerting him to someone coming up on his left. The boots barely pressed into the dirt, making almost no noise at all, but Stone reveled in the fact that he could finally sense Niccoli creeping up on him.

"Do try to be subtle," Niccoli said in his ear.

Stone frowned. "What do you mean?"

"You look like you're about to draw your sword, idiot," Niccoli hissed, his voice barely a whisper.

Stone nodded and tried to relax his face, but the anticipation still clawed at his gut. Pressure built in his chest, begging to be released with a scream as he fought to contain himself.

A wooden board creaked overhead, as if someone had stepped hard on a floorboard. Stone could imagine the network of bridges and houses in the treetops, but he only caught sight of bits here and there. In the emerald darkness cast by the leaves above, he couldn't see much of anything.

The road curved to the right and, once past the bend, a mansion popped into view. Its white paint offered a reprieve from the darkness and almost reflected light from it, illuminating the ground at its base. The dirt road ended in double doors, the frame painted with gold that glimmered in the candlelight from the lanterns. White walls rose into the treetops, every window framed in gold, the glass glowing with a light within each room. Stone couldn't even see the roof.

Two paths had been cut into the woods on either side of the mansion, leading to other, smaller homes of the isen master's children. He eyed the one to the left, grateful for the clear walkway, as it would take him to his escape.

Between the close-knit trees and thick underbrush,

they didn't stand a chance against the rebellion. He suppressed the impulse to grin. Burning them out would be almost too easy.

The mansion's front doors swung open and banged against the outer walls. Sconces mounted to the walls cast flickering light over a red carpet and a hallway wide enough for four men to stand side by side. Men and women lined the hall, all of them facing the entrance with smiles that left creases around their mouths and eyes. The strain etched into their fore-heads reminded Stone of a face he'd make if a knife were held to his back. He shuddered.

A bald man with the gut of two men strode from the mansion, his boots clapping along the carpet without leaving a trace of mud. His white shirt tucked into his black pants, he waved his hands in welcome. Every finger held at least one gold ring set with jewels. A beard he probably hadn't combed in months jutted from his face and hid his neck.

Niccoli strode forward and bowed. "It is good to see you, master."

"What have you brought me, boy?" Bakit asked.

A vein appeared in Niccoli's brow, and Stone allowed a small smirk through his façade.

"Wine to celebrate our two hundred years together," Niccoli said. He waved a hand toward the carts.

"Good. What else?"

"Slaves, dried meats, and gold."

Bakit nodded. "It will do. Let's sample that wine, shall we?"

Four men in beige slacks and shirts appeared behind Bakit and trotted out to the carts. With a few whip cracks, the horses snorted and pulled their carts toward the path on the right. Stone stepped back to allow them through.

Niccoli's slaves followed the carts without an order to guide them. They knew their chore: they would help pass the wine to everyone, soldiers and revelers alike. Stone avoided any eye contact as they passed in the hope none of them sent any knowing glances his way. He didn't need to arouse suspicion, not when he was so close.

"Come, come," Bakit said. He returned to the hall and strode in, with Niccoli in tow. Stone joined them, and the rest of Niccoli's isen followed. Stone took a deep breath to steady himself, but he took solace that these men wouldn't stand in his way during his escape. Only Stone and Niccoli had their own flasks from which to drink; the rest would fall asleep with the others to avoid suspicion. Andor had been left to guard the guild and wouldn't join them. It annoyed Stone that he cared enough to notice.

The hallway ended in a massive room filled with at least twenty tables barely a foot high. Metal plates and goblets marked the places on each surface, though he noticed a distinct absence of any forks or knives. Pillows rested on the floor in place of chairs, and Stone almost grimaced with annoyance. Barbarians.

Bakit sat with the force of a cannon, his belly fat jiggling as he came to rest on the pillow at the head of the center table. Niccoli sat to Bakit's right, and Stone curled his legs under him at the free space beside his master. Bakit snapped his fingers. A young girl in a beige skirt poured wine into a goblet by his plate, and he patted her rump in thanks. She cast her eyes to the floor and hurried away.

More women carrying flagons emerged from doors along the walls and began pouring wine into cups. Stone allowed one to be poured for himself. Bakit lifted his goblet, and those seated at the tables followed suit.

"To family!" Bakit said.

"To family!" the room chorused.

But instead of drinking, Bakit waited for the isen seated to take the first sips. Niccoli pressed his to his lips, and Stone did the same, but he held it there without drinking. He let the poison sit against his lip without allowing any to pass. Finally, when enough time had gone by, he set his cup again beside his plate.

Isen in the room turned to one another, chatting as more men and women in beige pants set ham and cheeses on their plates. Apparently satisfied at the lack of death, Bakit took a sip.

"Delicious," he said.

"Thank you," Niccoli said with a nod.

"Who made this wine?" Bakit asked as he grabbed a chicken leg from his plate and bit in.

"My associate, Stone," Niccoli said with a nod in his direction.

Below the table, Stone tightened his hand into a fist to hide his annoyance. If they were found out, now, Stone would take the blame.

"Good lad," Bakit said. He took another gulp from the goblet and lifted it with a look at a passing serving girl.

Stone nodded in thanks but chose not to speak. He had to remain inconspicuous, and he tended to anger those around him when he spoke.

Someone down the table hiccupped, and laughter erupted from around him. Stone began eating his ham, lifting his head now and then to check on the patrons. Everyone in the room, save for Stone and Niccoli drank, lifting their cups whenever a serving girl walked by.

He counted the seconds, tallying each minute in his mind. Ten minutes passed, and several of the more intoxicated men allowed their eyes to droop. After fifteen minutes, the first man fell backward and snored, while those around him laughed.

"The lush!" Bakit said with a laugh. His words slurred. He hadn't taken note of Niccoli's slow consumption, likely because his head had already begun to buzz and blur. Stone nodded to himself, content with the reactions thus far. An isen beside the sleeping man chuckled and poured wine on him, apparently to prove their master's point. He didn't stir.

Stone continued counting and picking at his food.

Boots squeaked on the polished floor. Stone turned in his seat to see a young man in slaves' slacks walk into the room behind him from a side hallway. He nodded to Stone and stood at the entrance, waiting for his command to begin the rebellion while Niccoli likely thought he'd come to await more orders.

As Stone expected, Niccoli kept his attention on Bakit. His eyes only left the man to examine his plate for a few seconds before they returned to his prey.

Within thirty minutes, a quarter of the room had fallen asleep. And within an hour, two-thirds of the room either leaned against the wall or lay on the floor. Aside from Niccoli's army, only a handful of Bakit's men and Bakit himself still sat upright.

Stone suppressed a groan of frustration. The fat man would be the last to go, and his nerves couldn't take much more of this waiting.

Bakit hiccupped and lifted his still-full glass for a refill, slurring as he spoke. "Girl... girl... more ..."

It was almost time.

Stone tilted his head out of Niccoli's line of vision

and caught the slave's eye. He nodded, and the man in beige slacks grinned. He retreated into the hallway.

Bakit burped and slumped backward, head smacking on the table with a thump that shook plates and knocked over half-empty goblets. Wine dripped onto the floor as he snored louder than any other man in the room, his great belly lifting and falling with each breath.

Niccoli tensed his arms as if to stand, but Stone set a hand on his shoulder. "Not yet."

"He's asleep!" Niccoli snapped under his breath.

"They aren't," Stone said, gesturing to a pair of men across the table. They caught his eye and lifted their glasses, eyes out of focus as they toasted nothing.

Niccoli pushed Stone's hand away. "They're too drunk to notice."

"We've come this far. Be patient," Stone said. He wasn't ready for Niccoli to do the deed, not yet. He had to wait for—

A whiff of smoke sailed past his nose, and he bristled. Not yet, fools. Not yet. He hoped Niccoli wouldn't notice. Perhaps he was too consumed with Bakit to say anything.

"What's that smell?" Niccoli asked, lifting his chin to sniff the air.

Damn.

Glass crashed in the distance. Someone yelled.

Niccoli pushed himself to his feet, and it took all of Stone's restraint not to curse in frustration. He couldn't let Niccoli think of anything but Bakit. He needed to be consumed with the master's death or else he might notice Stone's escape.

Glass shattered outside the house, and fire erupted at the nearest window. Niccoli stepped back. "What …"

"What's going on?" Stone asked, pretending he didn't know as he pushed himself to his feet.

"There's fire everywhere!" Niccoli spat.

None of Niccoli's men were awake to draw their swords or defend their master, but Niccoli had wriggled out of worse trouble—and he usually dragged Stone along with him. Stone had to play his cards right or this would crumble beneath him.

"An attack?" Niccoli asked.

Stone nodded. "Must be. If—"

"It doesn't matter," Niccoli said under his breath. He unsheathed a dagger from his waist and walked to his master, who still snored on the floor.

Good. Now for the next stage of his plan. Stone only had one chance to get away without Niccoli's notice, and he needed a good excuse to walk away. But it required an elaborate lie and fake interest in his master's wellbeing.

He pointed out the window. "We're not going to get out of this, Niccoli. We need to go, now. I don't know what's going on, but this isn't what we planned."

Niccoli knelt at his master's body and grinned without answering.

"Niccoli!" Stone pressed.

"Go check the exit. I'll be there shortly. Go!" his master snapped.

Stone almost smiled at his luck. He'd been about to suggest the same thing.

He obeyed, running out into the hall and shifting with each step. Flakes of skin flew behind him as he tore along the red carpet, changing into the Hillsidian who would carry him far from this place.

He blew past the door, leaving it open for the rebellion to make its way inside, and ran with the added speed of the Hillsidian body. His legs pumped beneath him, faster than he'd ever run before. His eyes scanned the night, snapping between shadows as the fires around the mansion grew taller. He tore through the side road and ran into the underbrush, far away from any guards who might still be awake. Brambles tugged at his shirt, tearing any cloth they grabbed.

But his luck didn't hold.

A bolt of fire flew past him and singed his shoulder. Pain rippled in his neck, and the singe of melted cloth choked his nose. He cried out in surprise but pressed onward as another bolt of fire missed him by inches.

Screams echoed through the wood, but he'd already gotten himself far enough away that he didn't see the carnage. Someone yelled overhead, and the fireballs stopped. Seconds later, something crunched nearby with all the force of a body hitting the forest floor.

A lichgate appeared not far off in the growing darkness, nothing more than two interlocking branches between a pair of trees. A bright field glimmered through the portal, teasing him with a taste of freedom. Stone jumped through it, and the familiar flare of blue light accompanied the twist in his gut as he entered another part of Ourea.

His legs carried him forward without any need for a path. He ran with everything he had, propelling himself through lichgate after lichgate, running through streams along the way to help hide his scent. His breath hitched, and pains shot along his core, but he never slowed. His only pauses came when he rushed to cover his tracks or to further disguise a few of the lichgates.

Stone ran with every ounce of strength he possessed, knowing more than his freedom was at stake. Even if he made it out of Niccoli's grasp this time, he could still be captured in the future. He would still have to find a way to break the bond, but at least for now he could escape the chains that had held him at Niccoli's side for so long.

And he was oh so very close.

Stone rested his hands on his knees and did his best not to vomit.

He sucked in air as fast as he could, but he had to rest. He had to pause for at least one second. Still fighting to catch his breath, he leaned back and cracked his neck, hands on his head as he took in the landscape past the final lichgate.

The amber glow of a sunset cast shadows over a forest on the horizon. The mountain under his feet gave him a view unlike any he'd ever seen—forests on every side of him bled away into the distance as the sunset scorched their leaves. A field stretched below him, accessible only via a twenty-minute hike down a narrow trail. Wheat bent in the wind. Despite several trails carved through the tall grasses by deer and other animals, he'd been smart enough to take one of the created routes, rather than forge his own.

He smiled and leaned against a boulder just off the path. He'd continue after a moment and a few more breaths.

Despite an ache burning in his thighs, he pushed forward and trotted along the trail. It leveled after a few minutes. Grasses sprung up alongside the path, and pine trees cast shade to relieve him from the burning sun. The mountain rock gave way to another clearing, this one about the size of Bakit's mansion and surrounded by a thin line of trees.

In its center, a gray rock jutted from the grass, a landmark he'd become familiar with as he studied the maps over the years. He headed for it, and sure enough, a small cottage rested in its shadow, tucked into a large groove in the mountain. Rock jutted all around it, surrounding the house on three sides.

Stone stumbled up to the front door and let himself in. The knob creaked. He took measured breaths to control his breathing, and with time, it became easier. He took in the cabin, studying his new home.

A single room filled most of the first floor, its walls covered with wooden panels. A stove and sink basin filled the right wall, both the color of the mountain rock. A wooden table sat beside a brick fireplace. Logs sat in the hearth, ready for him to light if need be, though he couldn't imagine doing so in this heat.

This was it. His haven. And Vivienne had spared nothing in preparing it for his new life.

A black door in the back of the cabin caught his eye. He opened it to reveal a bed covered with a blue blanket and a single wall lined from floor to ceiling with a giant bookcase. All of the books and maps he'd hidden only filled one shelf, but it would be enough of a start for his collection. He wished he'd been able to steal Udrenit's impressive selection, but those were likely long gone by now.

He frowned, realizing something—someone—was missing.

Vivienne.

The void burned within him, sudden and strong. He'd been so consumed with his escape that he hadn't even given her a thought, much less searched for her beacon. But she was supposed to join him. Where could she be? She wasn't here. She wasn't even anywhere nearby.

He stared at the floor, realization dawning on him like a slow sunset. A shiver threatened his neck, tickling the hairs there, but he suppressed it as he came to terms with a simple fact he'd overlooked.

She'd left him.

A brush of wind sailed past him from the still-open front door. He slammed the bedroom door behind him, and movement on the bed caught his eye. A small square of folded parchment shifted in the gust, sliding along the comforter. He lifted and opened it.

Good luck.

—V

He sat on the bed, the parchment in his hand the last connection to the woman who had become his weakness. That must have been what she'd been debating when he first introduced the plan. She was wondering if he would be distracted enough to let her escape. She'd used his plan against him.

Stone took a deep breath, his heart finally settled from his sprinting. She was gone without a trace, and he doubted she would return this time. Setting up the cottage, helping him in his escape—those were her parting gifts to him. He'd lost her.

He nodded and stood. Good. He didn't need that kind of weakness in his life again. He tossed the note on top of the logs in the fireplace. He'd burn her note when winter came. The itch still burned in his chest, but there was nothing he could do about the void now. It would never fill again.

But he'd made it. He'd lost Vivienne in the process, but he couldn't blame her. She wanted what he wanted, and they'd both finally found it.

He stared out the front window, eyes on the forests and fields below as he settled into the silence of the farmhouse. A bird twittered nearby, sharp and clear. Stone waited. He waited for Niccoli to charge through the lichgate and across the field below. He waited for his plan to fail, for everything to unravel. But with each passing second of silence, he began to wonder if he could truly win against Niccoli. Perhaps, he could break the bond, but for now he was living on borrowed time. He would not be welcomed back to Niccoli's guild; he would either be dragged back in chains or killed on sight.

Stone unbuckled the sword at his waist and held it

in his hands. He would save Niccoli the trouble if he was found and finally use this sword. Until then, he had experiments to run.

He threw the sword on the floor and grinned. It was time to find test subjects.

17

NEW EXPERIMENTS

March, 1002 A.D.
Wales, Kingdom of England

Stone walked along a dirt path in England, a basket of bread and dried beef in one hand. He shuffled along the soil, inching his way down a hill as he returned home. For eight years, Stone had explored Ourea and studied its energy, employing the one clue Death had given him in his pursuit of understanding. And for eight years, he flinched at sudden movements and snapping twigs in the dark, ever-terrified that Niccoli would find him.

Each year, he grew more and more frustrated with his experiments.

Death had told Vivienne—curse that Frenchwoman for leaving him—that everything was energy. If he understood the energy of Ourea, he reasoned, perhaps, he could one day break the bond that enslaved him to Niccoli.

But last year, he'd gotten an idea.

Lichgates seemed to breathe life into their environment. Anywhere he found a lichgate, it was overrun with plant life. Ivy, bushes, ancient trees—any time he studied the space around a lichgate, he found an abundance of life. If lichgates could breathe life into a space, perhaps they could do more.

His mind wandered into new territory as he pushed the boundaries of what he could comprehend, and he often imagined Vivienne scoffing with disgust as his experiments grew more daring. It didn't take long before he wondered what effect a lichgate would have on an unborn child. It made sense, in his mind, to question this—to grow a child near an epicenter like this could give it immense power. And if lichgates could give the ungifted energy and magic, perhaps they could also be instrumental in taking it away.

He'd desperately wanted to run his test on an unawaken isen, but he couldn't take the risk. A human was easier to find, and he doubted many more unawaken isen existed in either world. He had to study what was accessible to him for now, and he suspected these results would prove interesting.

It also intrigued him that the beacon was so much stronger on Earth than in Ourea, and he supposed it was because Ourea had more magical energy. There was interference, and it seemed to seep into Earth through the lichgates. That led to an all-important question: what would happen if he took a human with no magical gifts and raised it near a lichgate into Ourea? It offered so many possibilities he stayed awake at night wondering which would help him most. He rarely slept anymore, and he didn't mind.

His simple plan didn't take long to implement. He'd built a one-room house between two nearby lichgates, using each lichgate as a door into the home. He'd dared to go into England and risk discovery to persuade a pregnant, young Englishwoman with no home to partake in his experiment, and he fed her as promised. She hadn't asked questions, and he suspected she didn't care. She'd come willingly and, as long as he fed her well and kept her safe, she assured him she wouldn't leave. She never mentioned the child's father, and Stone could do without her story. He cared only to see what happened to the child as it grew.

The forest twittered with birdsong, and the branches rustled with life. He'd examined all these creatures already, and he wished for something new to learn. They jumped and ran about the canopy, basking in the filtered sunlight from the emerald leaves above and lived to eat and reproduce. Nothing new.

His lichgate appeared around a bend, and he smirked with self-satisfaction. It was nothing more than a door nailed between two trees, but the hinges shimmered despite the low light of the forest. He'd converted an existing lichgate to a door, and he counted that among his greatest accomplishments to date.

Stone twisted the handle and let himself in. The musky rust of copper hit him first, followed by a sour twist to the scent that reminded him of rotted cheese. He held a hand to his mouth and set the basket on the floorboards, closing the door as he studied the room for the source of the stench.

The English brunette lay on his bed along the far wall, her hair splayed out behind her. He frowned with disappointment and eyed her bed, which lay to his right—untouched. His blankets covered her, and her pale skin almost glowed white in the sunlight streaming through the window above the mattress. She didn't move, and her chin stuck into the air, neck exposed.

He inched forward, but the smell grew as he neared. A small bit of the blanket moved, wriggling over her still body.

Stone kept one hand to his mouth to mask the smell and instead breathed in the dried sweat stuck to the cloth. He tried to piece together what had happened. He'd barely been gone a day, and even then, he'd only left to get food. He hadn't wanted to miss the birth, to ensure the child lived.

Perhaps, he'd failed.

He pulled back the blanket to reveal pools of blood in the folds of her dress. The smell intensified, clawing at his nose and throat as if it fed off his agony. He gagged again and replaced the blanket.

The covers twitched again, this time by her waist. Stone lifted it to reveal her pale arm curved around a bundle of skin and brown hair. A white face peered back at him, small despite its wide eyes.

The child. She must have given birth while Stone was out. He frowned, disappointed that she hadn't survived to care for the child during his experiments.

The baby cooed. It reached a little hand for him, its fingers stretching as it watched him. Studied him. Something stirred in Stone's chest. The void that had burned within him since Vivienne left itched a little less when this tiny creature looked at him that way.

He lifted the child in his hands. Its skin stuck to him, coated in a layer of goo. He grimaced but held it regardless. A boy. It continued to watch him with those wide eyes, and he wondered why it wasn't crying. Usually these things sobbed buckets, but not this one.

It giggled and reached for his nose.

A memory popped into his mind from ages back: the first memory he'd seen in that guard's mind. Chad. He'd been a child, and his father had raised his fist often to strike him when he sobbed.

Stone pursed his lips. Perhaps Chad's soul hadn't

been a complete waste after all. Stone knew how to raise a broken man, and he could avoid doing so with this infant. Though he hadn't intended on raising a child—only studying the effect of lichgates on it throughout its life—perhaps Stone could turn this boy into something useful.

A piece of paper on the table caught Stone's eye, and he leaned toward it to read. Letters scribbled across the paper in barely legible script he didn't recognize.

Girl—Callie. Boy—Cedric.

The mother's last words. Funny, he didn't know she could write or read. He frowned. Perhaps even she hadn't suspected she would survive.

Stone took a deep breath despite the foul stench of the cabin. "Well, Cedric, I suppose you'll need to be made presentable. We have lots of work to do."

The baby giggled, and the void in Stone's chest filled a little more at the sound.

IMPORTANT CHARACTERS AND TERMS

🜚

MAIN CHARACTERS

Kara Magari - Born in our world but dragged into Ourea by fate, Kara Magari was raised a human but soon finds out she's much more as she becomes the second Vagabond and master of the powerful Grimoire.

Braeden Drakonin - A Stelian Heir raised as a Hillsidian orphan, Braeden loathes his heritage and rejects his lineage. When he meets Kara he thinks he's found a way to officially leave behind his past and start a fresh life free from his cruel father.

❧

OTHER CHARACTERS BY KINGDOM

HILLSIDE

The Hillsidian race is most similar to humans in appearance. Hillsidian blood is green.

Notable Hillsidian Characters:

Gavin - Heir of Hillside. Cunning, aggressive, and a bit of a womanizer. Raised as Braeden's brother.

Richard - King to the Blood Lorraine, ruler of Hillside and Gavin's mother. He and Gavin don't have much of a relationship.

Twin - A palace servant and close friend to Kara Magari.

Blood Lorraine - Ruler of Hillside. Mother to Gavin and adoptive mother of Braeden.

AYAVEL

The Ayavelian race is characterized by the triple irises in their eyes.

Notable Ayavelian Characters:

Blood Aislynn - Blood of Ayavel. She has spent her life brokering peace between the kingdoms and has, to some degree, succeeded. She has no children or Heirs of her own.

Evelyn - Blood Aislynn's niece and chosen ruler of Ayavel upon her aunt's death.

KIRELM

Kirelm people live high above the ground in a kingdom that floats over the Rose Cliffs and therefore have wings to travel.

Notable Kirelm Characters:

Aurora - Daughter to Blood Ithone and Heir to the kingdom, though she is the first female Heir in their kingdom's history. Their culture celebrates men as the leaders of the race, rather than women, and this has been a great shame to her father.

Blood Ithone - Ruler of Kirelm. Set in the ways of his culture, he has always been disappointed that he did not have a son to call his heir.

STELE

Stelians have grey skin and smoke steaming from their pores. They can change form to mimic other yakona races.

Notable Stelian Characters:

Blood Carden - A cruel ruler with a vendetta against the other kingdoms. He has worked tirelessly his entire life to get revenge, and he's so very, very close.

Queen Myra - Blood Carden's murdered wife and Braeden's mother. There's more to her death than meets the eye, and Braeden is determined to get his revenge.

LOSSE

Lossians can breathe under water which comes in handy since the kingdom of Losse is beneath the sea in a protective bubble.

Notable Lossian Characters:

Blood Frine - The careful, cunning, and manipulative ruler of Losse. He prefers to keep to his isolated kingdom and let the other kingdoms war with each other.

ISEN

Isen are soul stealers. By stealing a soul every decade or so they can stay young forever, but at a cost: the more souls they possess within them, the more likely they are to lose their minds. Isen can take the form of the souls they steal and impersonate their victims. A small retractable barb in their wrist is inserted into the neck of their victims in order to capture their soul.

Notable Isen Characters:
　　Deidre
　　Niccoli
　　Agneon

DRENOWITH

The Drenowith are also known as muses. These immortal creatures are very difficult to kill and have the ability to take the form of any creature, but they cannot reproduce. It's said they've been around since the first days of the Earth and prefer to be left to their own devices. Their magic is the cause of many, if not most natural disasters.

Notable Drenowith Characters:

Adele

Garrett

Verum

Mirrow

KINGDOMS AND NOTABLE PLACES OF OUREA

Hillside - A beautiful maze of trees. The castle itself isn't made from stone or dead wood, but is rather comprised of the five largest trees in the kingdom, all of which sit in the middle of the sprawling city. Those who live and work in the castle use the hundreds of rope bridges to cross between the rooms hollowed out of the trunks. It's a green paradise and a kingdom ruled by the Hillsidian Blood. Brilliant walkways span out from the castle like rays on a sun, the paths covered in shifting stones that take the shape of whatever touches them.

Ayavel - A kingdom of light ruled by the Ayavelian Blood. Ayavelians have the rare ability to shapeshift into any of the other yakona, as long as they practice early in life. Their natural skin is iridescent, glimmering like diamonds, and they possess eyes with three irises in them that can each convey subtly different emotions. The Kingdom of Ayavel is surrounded by a tall, white wall that protects the kingdom. The city is comprised mainly of white buildings trimmed with gold that have domed roofs and towering golden spires. The roads are lined with cherry blossom trees and their petals fly through the air with the breeze.

Kirelm - In the clouds somewhere near the Rose Cliffs of Ourea, the kingdom of Kirelm floats above the surface. Two layers of intricate and impenetrable wires keep intruders out while allowing the sunlight in. The silver-skinned people of this kingdom are equipped with massive wings in shades of white, gray, and black which allow them to travel throughout this kingdom in the sky ruled by the Kirelm Blood.

The Stele - A dark and dangerous place, the Stele is a

home to many of Ourea's most terrifying creatures. Long ago banished from the other yakona realms, the Stelians are a culture of outcasts who resent their centuries of banishment. Like the Ayavelians, Stelians possess the ability to shape-shift, but their true form is the stuff of nightmares. Their ash-gray skin spews smoke when they're angry, and there are no whites to their eyes. The Stelian Blood rules over this kingdom.

Losse - This underwater kingdom is only accessible to those who can breathe underwater or those who are able to take the sting of the magical starfish that temporarily filters air from the water long enough to reach the kingdom's gate. Once in the protective golden bubble that encompasses the kingdom with air, the starfish is no longer needed . . . unless you want to leave, that is. Lossians have blue skin and large seaweed-green eyes. Most of them are bald, but some have black hair. Their thin form and webbed feet help them swim to their kingdom while breathing under-water. The Lossian Blood is the ruler of this kingdom.

The Villing Caves - Once a celebrated haven of caverns and lakes, the Villing Caves became the resting place for the Retriens. The long-lost yakona kingdom had claimed this place as their own after the fall of Ethos, but a dragon invasion soon thinned them out. In a last-ditch effort to protect his people, the Retrien Blood had no choice but to seal himself and the dragons into the caves. However, his Heir did not awaken as the new Blood, and so it's believed that the Blood still lives trapped inside the stone.

The Vagabond's Village - The Vagabond's Village is where the first vagabond and his followers lived. The Vagabond himself lived in a lavish mansion surrounded by the beautiful stone cottages his followers lived in, all of which was safely tucked away in a wooded valley. There is only one way to enter. First, visitors must get past the Lyth before attempting to pass through the terrifying Amber Temple, a place of worship which long ago opened a portal to deadly demons that took over the surrounding area. These creatures can only be contained by a glowing magical hourglass, but be warned: if the sands within are moving, the demons are trapped; but as soon as the last grain falls, they are free again.

Ethos - The abandoned city of Ethos is where all the yakona races once lived in unity and peace. There is little facts still known about its fall, but it's said the Stelians were at fault and that is, at least in part, the cause for their banishment. It was the First Vagabond's goal to reunite the kingdoms once more and rebuild Ethos.

GLOSSARY

Yakona - The yakona are one of the peoples of Ourea and known to be true masters of magic. Over eons, the six races have evolved to look quite different from each other: the Ayavelians, the Stelians, the Hillsidians, the Kirelms, the Lossians, and the Retrien.

Bloods and Heirs - Bloods are the rulers of each yakona kingdom, given the right to rule by unique magic in their blood that's passed from parent to child. The Bloods are connected to their subjects through a shared blood connection, which allows them to control the actions of their people via mandates and blood-bound orders. Heirs possess a lesser version of the blood magic, though Bloods and Heirs heal almost instantly from a wound. Upon a Blood's death, the Heir awakens and takes on the powers of his or her predecessor. The awakening is an incredibly painful process, thought to be the most painful experience known.

Sartori - Sword belonging to the Blood of each race. Only the Blood can wield the sword as touching the hilt will burn anyone else. The entire blade is coated with the only known poison that can kill a Blood, and each Sartori has a slight variation of the poison. An antidote can be made, but only from the blade that caused the wound.

The Grimoire - The First Vagabond created the Grimoire to document everything he knew about Ourea so that it could be passed down. The magical book can flip its own pages, make drawings come to life, and so much more.

The Vagabond's Necklace - The four-leaf clover pendant has a stone in the middle. It's able to hide the Grimoire from sight so that those who seek the power within cannot steal it. The stone can be clear, which means the Grimoire isn't magically hiding within the stone, or blue, which means it is. Only the Vagabond can call the book forward or wish it away.

Blood Loyalty - Each kingdom has a ruler called a Blood. The Blood can control the people in their kingdom through the blood loyalty. Anyone given a silent or spoken command must follow it. Cedric, the First Vagabond, discovers that he does not have a blood loyalty, and therefore does not need to follow commands given by his blood.

Lichgates - A lichgate is a portal that ties our world to the terrifying and beautiful world of Ourea. Lichgates can be found in remote places, and when you walk through a lichgate, the land you cross into is not what you would see if you'd simply walked around the portal. There are also lichgates within Ourea that can make traveling vast distances easier... if you know where they are.

Ethos - Ethos is an ancient city which once housed all the races of Ourea in one place. They lived in harmony until it was discovered that a Stelian figured out a way to steal the bloodline from other yakona royal families. After that, Stelians were banished and trust between the yakona races eroded. They all went their separate ways and abandoned Ethos.

YOU'RE MISSING OUT...

Boyce posts official artwork, updates, and random things that will make you laugh on Facebook, Instagram, and Twitter.

Boyce also created a special Facebook group specifically for readers like you to come together and share their lives and interests, especially regarding the Grimoire Saga novels. Please check it out and join in whenever you get the chance! Everyone in there is amazing, and you'll fit right in.

https://www.facebook.com/groups/Grimoire-Readers/

Sign up for email alerts of new releases AND exclusive access to the Grimoire Saga Fandom Encyclopedia: the official guide to Ourea exclusively for the Grimoire Saga's biggest fans. The encyclopedia is

ONLY available to Boyce's VIP email tribe, so sign up now to get access:

https://smboyce.com/email-signup-pages/grimoire-saga/

Enjoying the series? Awesome! Help others discover the Grimoire Saga by leaving a review at Amazon: **http://mybook.to/misanthrope**

BOOKS BY S. M. BOYCE

The Grimoire Saga

Lichgates

Treason

Heritage

Illusion

The Misanthrope

The First Vagabond: Rise of a Hero

The First Vagabond: Fall of a Legend

The Demon

The Fairhaven Chronicles

Glow

Shimmer

Ember

Nightfall

Standalone Novels

Ari

ACKNOWLEDGMENTS

This novel would be wordier if not for my knock-your-socks-off editor, Allisyn Ma. Thank you, also, to Ginny Gallagher for combing through the book one last time in a final proofread. And thank you to my talented formatter, J. Scott Sharp, for making the books look so pretty.

Big hug to my beta readers—J. N. Chaney & Dad— for letting me throw this at you in the final minutes.

Also, special thanks to Lika and Seb, the amazing people who know multiple languages and helped me make this book more realistic.

And of course, my content editor/husband is a talented man who daydreams with me and is brutally honest if he thinks something sucks. Thank you, Geoff, despite my occasional wincing.

ABOUT THE AUTHOR

S. M. Boyce is a lifelong writer with a knack for finding adventure and magic. Known for enchanting, expansive, and epic worlds, Boyce writes action-packed adventures with heroes who push boundaries to make their worlds better.

Word-of-mouth is crucial for any author to succeed. If you enjoyed this novel, please consider leaving a review at Amazon, even if it's only a line or two. Your review will make all the difference and is hugely appreciated.